To J,

*Journey to the French
River with Grace &
her friends.*

*Gillian
Feb, 2017*

River *of the*
Stick Wavers

GILLIAN ANDREWS

◆ FriesenPress

Suite 300 - 990 Fort St
Victoria, BC, V8V 3K2
Canada

www.friesenpress.com

ISBN
978-1-4602-8935-8 (Hardcover)
978-1-4602-8936-5 (Paperback)
978-1-4602-8937-2 (eBook)

1. *FICTION, CONTEMPORARY WOMEN*

Distributed to the trade by The Ingram Book Company

I dedicate this book to all women.
You are stronger than you think.

This is one woman's journey.

Acknowledgements

There are many people who have made this novel possible. In no particular order, I would like to thank my editor, Sara Saddington. You challenged me to think deeply about my story. You encouraged me when I questioned my abilities. In the end, you made me a better writer. To my son, Simon, for listening to all my concerns about this book. You helped me to figure things out when I was struggling. I especially want to thank you for asking me if you could read the first draft. I never expected it, but I was thrilled all the same. Then there is Helen Tyndall, who introduced me to the French River. I fell in love with it instantly. You were also one of the first people to read my book and give me feedback, along with Joan Weller, Gwen Robinson, and my daughter, Mallory. You were all so patient whenever I talked about how my story was progressing and offered your insights. I also want to thank Norman Dokis, for putting up with my emails asking questions about Native life on the Dokis Reserve at the French River. Thanks also to Cecil Isaac, of Walpole Island, for agreeing to read about the sweat lodge ceremony to check it for accuracy, and for sharing your own experiences of a sweat ceremony. To Mia Saddington. You always believed in me. You dove right in to help me to plan the launch party for this book. Your business acumen and organizational skills will help to make it happen. To Justin Teeuwen, a writer and motivational speaker in his own right, who did such a beautiful job on my author photo. And finally, to my husband, Wayne, for the freedom to dream, and for your support in making my publishing dream come true. You are my friends, my family, my support, and kindred spirits. I love you all.

Blessings.

River of the Stick Wavers

Early May 1963

Grace Irwin's motor boat seemed to know its way to the camp on the French River. For that reason, she didn't worry about veering off her path. Instead, she enjoyed the sensation of the river, as it rustled beneath her. The cool May breeze seemed to carry away the stress of the past two months. It felt good to get away from the city, from the memories, and the pain of grieving.

An icy spray of water on her hand brought her back to the present. When she looked around, she saw a carved wooden sign swinging in the breeze. Crow's Nest, on Four Mile Island, was to be her home until the end of August. The camp was nestled in a copse of fir trees that had miraculously grown out of the rocky surface of the Pre-Cambrian Shield. As promised by the owners, the floating dock was already in the water awaiting her arrival.

Grace's boat slid into the dock with a gentle bump. She had to fight to gain her balance when she stepped onto the shifting dock. She secured the boat and made her way to stable ground. There was a bit of a sandy beach that had been brought in by the owners, but mostly there was nothing but granite all around. Pine trees grew on both sides of the camp. And there seemed to be some kind of shed on one side. She'd check that out later. For now, she carried her supplies, one by one, to the camp situated on a gentle rise.

When the final load had been retrieved, she took a moment to sit on the bottom step of the deck to rest her head. She closed her eyes as memories came flooding back. Long summer days spent on the French River had been her happiest time as a child. She listened to the sounds that were indicative of camp life. The river, the birds, and even the land beneath her feet, were music to her ears. She opened her slate grey eyes upon a landscape that she hoped would heal her shattered spirit. The sight energized her and gave her strength. She planned to remain at the camp until Labour Day weekend. An unusually long time, she knew, but she had no reason to hurry home. Besides, she needed the time to figure out what to do with her life now that her husband was gone. She went inside to unpack.

Grace's shoes echoed on the plank-wood floor, as she made her way to the small kitchen. The miss-matched cupboards and ancient appliances looked serviceable, she decided. Once the kitchen was stocked, she went into the only bedroom that looked out over the river. She unpacked a flannelette nightgown, which she lay on the bed. She placed her book, journal, and her favourite pen, on the rustic bedside table. Her toiletries went in the bathroom. That just left her clothes. But she'd take care of them later. There was something she had to do first. It had been too many years since she had been able to visit this river. She wanted to watch the sun go down before she turned in for the night.

On her way out the door, she grabbed an afghan off the chair by the window. She also remembered to leave the outside light on to guide her way back. Being alone as she was, she couldn't afford to be stumbling around in the dark.

Grace sighed as she lowered herself into the Adirondack chair and contemplated her love for this ancient river. A river that once drained east toward Lake Nipissing, but for the tilting landscape, now drained west into Georgian Bay. Her connection to this river began as a child during family visits. Whenever she was away from it, it called to her. She knew she'd find some peace here, whereas in Toronto there were too many distractions. Though the river had changed direction with the shifting landscape, it had survived. Just as she must now survive her own shifting landscape.

She watched a young couple paddle by. The sound of their laughter floated across the water. She waved, but they were too wrapped up in each other to notice. She smiled to herself fondly. Even after all these years, she still remembered what it felt like to be in love. But that all came to an abrupt end on the first day of spring, when her husband died of a heart attack while walking across the university campus.

Grace was brought back to the present by a chill in the night air that seeped into her bones. The pine trees swayed with the wind, and dark clouds moved across the night sky. With hunched shoulders, the lone figure ambled back to camp.

Grace tugged the afghan around her shoulders as she leaned against the closed door. She walked over to the fireplace and set a match to the newspaper tucked beneath the kindling. Within minutes, she had a nice fire going. She held out her hands to the flames to warm them and surveyed the empty room. She really was alone here. If anything happened to her, no-one would know. They'd probably find her days from now, maybe even weeks, her body in decay. She shook her head to dispel the image from her mind. Maybe if she read a little. She retrieved her book from the bedroom and changed into her nightgown. Once on the couch, with her feet tucked beneath her, she tried to read. But every creak, every bang of a tree branch on the roof, disturbed her. She lay down in the hope that if she kept her eyes closed long enough she'd be able to sleep.

Thunder roared and lightening shot across the sky, lighting up the place on the couch, where a frightened Grace lay huddled. She pulled the afghan over her head, but that didn't keep away the images of Charles that flashed through her mind. Like when their eldest son, Chuck, had the whooping cough, Charles had insisted on taking care of their son. Then there was his patience with Jack for skipping school, because he neglected to study for a math test.

And she would never forget his cold lifeless body, as it lay with so much finality, in his solitary coffin. How could he be dead?

For weeks after his death, Grace expected him to come walking through the front door; that it had all been a bad dream. But she was alone. She was tired of being alone. Tired of being afraid. Most of all, she was angry with Charles for dying and leaving her to carry on without him.

Another crack of thunder made her shudder. She had no control over the elements. What's more, she had no control of whatever life sent her way. That frightened her even more. The fear made her angry. Fear of what? Fear of God? Fear of death? Fear of not having control? All of the above. There was a restless yearning for the life that had been turned upside down by a sudden twist of fate. Her right leg began to move with quick little jerky motions under the cover. A silent rage bubbled in her throat that refused to be released. Eyes wide, she sat up unable to breathe. Without knowing what she was doing, Grace tossed the cover aside and rushed out into the stormy night. She didn't care if she got struck by lightning, perhaps she even hoped for it, so she wouldn't have to hurt any more.

The hard rain stung as it plastered her nightgown to her body, but she was past caring. Grace railed at the heavens with both fists clenched. "Why? Why? Oh Why?" Emotions overwhelmed her with their intensity. Tears mingled with the rain, as she slid to her knees on the cold hard ground, where she allowed herself the full measure of her grief.

Grace had no idea how much time passed before she became aware of the cold. She trembled as the wind seeped past the flimsy barrier of her wet nightgown. She knew she had to move, but it was an effort to force her frozen limbs to submit to her will. Then over the driving rain and wind, she heard a sound coming from the river. She struggled to her feet and faced the storm that lashed her body. There it was again. She couldn't be certain, because it was broken by the wind, but it sounded like singing. She turned her head to one side to listen more carefully. But whatever she thought she heard, was gone now. It must be the wind playing tricks, she decided. She wrapped her arms around her frozen body and stiffly made her way back to the camp.

She went into her bedroom to replace her soaked nightgown with a white terry robe from her suitcase. Her body shivered and quaked, as she turned on the sauna in the bathroom. Then she headed to the kitchen to get a bottle of wine from the fridge. With shaky hands, she filled a juice glass half way and drank it. She felt its soothing warmth course through her body. She refilled the glass and carried it into the bathroom, where she placed it on a little stool. Still wrapped in her robe, she sat on a wooden bench and soaked up the warmth. She added water to the hot coals between bouts of tears. When she felt sufficiently warm, she crawled beneath the bed covers and slept more deeply than she had in months.

II

The morning sun shone through the bedroom window waking Grace from a deep dreamless sleep. She turned away from its relentless appeal to join the day in a vain attempt to recapture oblivion. Her thoughts began to jump from one thing to another, most notably to the events of the night before. She rolled onto her back and stared up at the bare ceiling. It reminded her of an empty canvas, much like herself. Now that was a daunting thought.

She slipped out of bed and headed to the kitchen, where she filled the coffee peculator with water from the tap. She scooped two tablespoons of coffee into a little basket attached to a long tube, positioned the whole inside the percolator, and secured the lid. The promising smell of perked coffee soon permeated the air.

Grace slid two pieces of bread into the toaster. She retrieved a plate and silverware from the cupboard, and the peanut butter and jam from the fridge, and placed them on a small table by the window. By the time she finished her second cup of coffee, she began to revive.

Until last night, she hadn't realized the depth of her sorrow. The storm must have triggered something inside her that helped to release her pent-up emotions. During Charles's funeral, everyone tried to do and say the right things. They all meant well, but nothing could ease the pain in her heart. The only thing that had kept her going was the need to be strong in the eyes of her two grown sons. Once they went back to their own lives, and all the people were gone, she was alone again. She didn't even have the solace of work to take her mind off her sorrow.

The raucous cry of birds, in the trees outside the window, reminded Grace that she was indeed at the French River. She had four months to figure things out.

For now, Grace was content to stay close to the camp. She found a hammock in the shed and hung it between two pine trees between the camp and the river. She wore her cable knit sweater for warmth and settled in the hammock to read her book, the *Feminine Mystique* by Betty Friedan. But her attention was caught by her surroundings. She watched the birds swoop and glide, until she became tired. With one foot on the ground, she set the hammock into motion. She was asleep before it stopped rocking.

The insistent tapping of a woodpecker against the tree trunk, shattered Grace's slumber. She reluctantly opened her eyes and tried to spy the noisy culprit, but it seemed to be well hidden in the trees.

After lunch, Grace wondered what she was going to do with herself for the rest of the day, when her attention was drawn to the small bookcase by the fireplace. Curiosity piqued, she went over to investigate what the previous residents had left behind. She flipped through the titles until she came across what appeared to be a journal. She felt funny reading someone else's private writings, but curiosity got the better of her, and she opened it to the first entry.

The writing was small, perhaps that of a woman, she guessed. The entries were dated 1922 and talked of a couple's time on the river. Grace became engrossed in the entries, until she became jealous of the time this unknown couple had spent together. It reminded her too much of her own widowed state. Would the rest of her life be spent alone and lonely, now that her husband was gone? The wound in Grace's heart was still tender. It was hard to be reminded that she would have to face the future without Charles. Throughout her entire life, someone had been there to take care of her. First her parents, then Charles. Even at school, there had been people to advise her and friends to whom she could confide.

After she got married, she lost touch with her friends. No, that wasn't quite true. She began to distance herself from her closest friends, when she was dating Charles. After all, boyfriends would come and go, but friends could always be counted on to be there when you needed them. Now she realized how naïve her thoughts had been.

Looking back, she could see that Charles's needs always came first. As a new wife, she had done all she could to please him. But as time went by, it became more difficult to accept her role as nothing more than wife and mother. But she was a product of her upbringing, as well as her environment, and so she tried to do her best. It wasn't always easy. Even her friends had been the wives of Charles's colleagues at the university. Now that he was gone, she didn't feel like she belonged with those people any more. She didn't know where she belonged. She'd come to the French River to find out. Was she running away from her life or toward a new one? The thought worried Grace. Despite that, she still wasn't about to go back to Toronto. She was paid up for the summer. She was going to make the best of it.

III

The following day, Grace decided it was time to venture farther afield. To bolster her confidence, she dressed in a pair of slim-fitting cream coloured pants, with a white blouse and flats, and went to visit the Trading Post. Her ash blonde hair, freshly washed in a perfectly coiffed bob, blew into her eyes as she propelled the motor boat across Dry Pine Bay. Once she entered the channel, it was necessary to slow down in order to maneuver through the swifts, before she could dock at the marina. From there, it was just a short walk, along a winding, tree-lined path, to the Trading Post.

The air was decidedly cooler in the dimly lit confines of the store. Once her eyes adjusted to the change in light, Grace could make out canned goods, coffee, and sugar stacked behind the worn wooden counter. A pungent smell filled her nostrils and drew her eyes to the end of the counter, where a fly hovered around a naked block of cheese sitting beside an equally bare cooked ham. A single knife, recently used, sat between the two. Large jars of candy shared counter space, and bins of vegetables crowded up against the counter on the rough-hewn floor.

"Is there anything I can get you Missus?"

"Oh you scared me." Grace turned and saw a stout little man with a bulbous nose and small beady eyes. He wore a short-sleeve checkered shirt and a pair of baggy pants beneath a dingy white apron.

He gave her the once over. "Henry Franco at your service."

Grace took a slight step back from the sweaty man. "I just came in to pick up a few things," she said holding up her list for him to see.

He reached out his beefy hand and said, "I'll take care of that. I know where everything is."

"Oh, all right," Grace said. "I guess I'll just wander around for a bit."

"Where do you hail from?" he asked.

"I'm visiting from Toronto," she answered. "I'm staying at Crow's Nest for the summer."

Mr. Franco paused in the middle of placing an item in a brown paper bag. His eyes became hooded, and his face turned a mottled red.

"Are you all right, Mr. Franco?" Grace asked, a look of concern on her face.

"Fine," he replied abruptly.

Afraid to intrude on Mr. Franco's mood, Grace walked deeper into the store to give him some privacy and herself some distance. His response to her remark about where she was staying made her a little nervous. It was as though he was upset with her. Perhaps she was being unkind, she decided. Maybe he was brusque with everyone.

When she walked down the center of the store, being careful not to run into the wood stove, she saw pots and pans hanging from the rafters, along with heavy blankets, rifles, fishing rods, and tools. Pictures of animals and landscapes lined the walls as well as novelty items for the tourists. She stopped to sort through a bin filled with Levi's. She needed something more serviceable to wear while she explored the area. To these she added a pair of canvas shoes, which she spied in a bin beside the moccasins.

When Grace returned to the counter with her purchases, she said, "Excuse me, Mr. Franco. Do you have anything that would suffice as a journal?" Hers was almost full.

"A journal? Folks around here make do with an old notebook," he uttered gruffly. He rooted around behind the counter, until he found what he was looking for, and tossed the item in question on the flat surface. "Anything else you'll be needing?"

"Is there anywhere I could try on these Levis?" she asked.

"Not it you don't mind doing it right where you're at," he smirked as he puffed on a fat cigar. The smoke concealed his eyes.

She blanched. Despite the smoke, she didn't miss his meaning. Perhaps her first impression of him had some merit, after all. "Never mind. These look like they'll fit. I'll take these canvas shoes as well."

Just as she was about to pay Mr. Franco what she owed him, Grace heard the doorbell jangle at the front of the store. Four teenage boys bounded in talking excitedly. They were all dressed uniformly, in Levis and a white t-shirt, which stood out against their dark colouring, and jet black hair.

She overhead them talking excitedly about a canoe trip they were taking. They reminded her of her own two boys when they were younger: all nervous energy and excitement.

"Here now, what do you want?" Mr. Franco demanded.

An uncomfortable silence filled the air.

"We just came in to pick up a few supplies," the oldest of the boys replied politely.

"Well, be quick about it. I don't reckon to the likes of you hanging around here."

Disconcerted by the man's unexpected hostility, Grace was uncertain how to react.

Seeing her discomfort, Mr. Franco said, "You're new around here Missus, so I'll have to educate you. Indians are nothing but a bunch of thieves. Not a one of them can be trusted."

"Surely that's not true?" she responded, struggling to assert herself.

He pointed a knobby finger at her. "Just stay away from them if you know what's good for you."

Grace shrank from the man's unexpected harsh words. She picked up her packages and headed for the door feeling properly chastised. She smiled shyly at the young men on her way out.

"You forgot your change," Mr. Franco called out.

* * * * * *

After her encounter with Mr. Franco, Grace needed to get out of the house to clear her head. As soon as she paired her newly purchased Levis with a heavy sweater, and the white canvas shoes she had purchased at the Trading Post, she was ready to take a walk over the rugged landscape behind the camp.

The island was covered with jack pines and red oak. Scrub brush abounded, and wildflowers of red, pink, white, and purple grew in profusion upon the ground. Could any place be as beautiful as this? She breathed in the fresh clean air and felt the events of the morning slip away.

She closed her eyes and listened. Leaves whispered through the trees, birds twittered, and the distant sound of the French rippled against the rock face. Even the chipmunks chattered incessantly, as they went about their daily business.

When she opened her eyes, Grace was startled by the sight of a lone rabbit in her field of vision. Once it sensed she was no threat, it hopped away.

When Grace spied an inviting path through a wooded area, she decided to follow it. She stepped carefully over fallen debris, then gasped when she reached the other side and realized she wasn't alone. "Oh, I didn't realize anyone else was here."

"Come here and tell me what you think of this," the strange woman said.

Grace moved cautiously toward the woman, who stepped to one side of an easel, where she was working on a landscape painting. "Is there a problem?" Grace asked, eyeing the painting.

"I don't know," the woman said. "I'm not sure if I've got the lighting quite right."

Grace looked at the way the sun hit the trees, then she looked back at the painting. "What time of day did you start this painting?" she asked.

"Of course," the woman admonished herself. "How foolish of me. Once I start painting, time just slips away. You know art?"

"Not really. My mother's the expert. But I do recall seeing a series of paintings by Claude Monet. He painted the same row of poplar trees at different times of the day. It was fascinating to see how light and shadow affect a painting. That's how I knew about the lighting," she shrugged.

"Oh yes, the Poplar series. I know it well," the woman said with some authority.

"You're familiar with Monet's work then?"

"You could say that. I spent some time at Giverny."

Grace was astounded. "How did you manage that? I didn't know they gave tours?"

"I was invited to visit the grounds with a group of artists."

"Oh my. Is it as beautiful as the paintings?" Grace asked.

"The paintings will always have their own story to tell," the woman responded. "Have you ever tried painting?"

"Once. But I'm afraid I'm not very good."

"Why do you say that?"

"I'm just not good with watercolours. The colours get all muddy."

Grace took in the other woman's masculine white shirt and twill pants. Her grey hair was cropped short on her angular face. And she had a no-nonsense manner about her which Grace found comforting. She was nothing like her mother. Grace liked her instantly.

"Where are my manners," the woman interrupted Grace's thoughts. "I haven't even introduced myself."

Grace chuckled. "I'm sorry. You're right, of course." She reached out her hand in greeting. "My name's Grace Irwin. I'm staying at the camp on the other side of those trees."

"Oh, you mean Crow's Nest." The woman wiped the paint from her hands and offered it to Grace. "Margaret Williams. Maggie to my friends. What do you say we continue this conversation over dinner? I don't know about you, but I'm hungry. I'm sure Albert is wondering where I've gotten to. Though he should be used to my wanderings by now."

"Albert?" Grace helped Maggie pack her supplies.

"Albert is my husband. We've been together for forty years," she smiled fondly. "Is there a mister in your life?"

"There was," Grace responded sadly. "Up until two months ago. My husband died."

"So you're here all alone?"

Grace nodded.

"Seems like Albert's been baking again," Maggie said when they arrived at her cottage. "It smells like oatmeal raisin. They'll be perfect for dessert."

Grace was impressed. Charles never baked. She would never have asked such a thing of him. He was the one who went to work all day, after all. Her job was to make sure things ran smoothly at home.

"Albert must be out," Maggie said when she returned from the extra bedroom, where she stashed her art supplies. "He did say he might check out the arbutus this afternoon."

"I beg your pardon?"

"The arbutus. You know, those pink and white blossoms that hide beneath low-lying branches?"

"Oh, is that what they are? I wondered what they were called."

"Albert is an amateur horticulturist. He often takes off to explore the flora on the island to see if he can discover a new species."

"You come here often?"

"My family has had a camp on Four Mile Island for as long as I can remember." Maggie smiled while she puttered around the kitchen. "We spend most of our summers here now."

"I can certainly understand why. When I was a child, my parents brought me here all the time. I've always loved it."

"Why did you stay away so long?"

"Charles, that's my husband, and I, always went abroad every summer. He taught history you see. He liked to explore it first-hand. Don't get me wrong, I enjoyed our trips too. It's just that sometimes I would have loved to do something less complicated. It would have been nice to share all of this with him," Grace said wistfully.

"Did you tell him that?"

"No. It was easier to just go where he wanted to. Now it's too late."

"Well, never mind. All that matters is that you're here now."

"I think someone is staying at the camp on the other side of the marsh," Albert said. He paused when he saw Grace sitting at the kitchen table. "Oh, I didn't know we had company."

"You must be Albert?" Grace stood to greet Maggie's husband. He put his big calloused hand into her smaller one. Red suspenders held up tan corduroys on his bony frame. His worn shirt was rolled up at the sleeves and exposed the sinewy arms of a man who was used to manual labour. His face was all angles with a large pointy nose, and his eyes twinkled with humour.

"And you must be our new neighbour," he smiled sheepishly.

They had a lovely meal of cold fried chicken and potato salad, with fresh baked bread and followed by Albert's delicious cookies.

"These cookies are wonderful," Grace said, helping herself to another. "Do you bake often?"

"Only if I don't want to starve to death," he smiled affectionately at his wife. "Maggie tends to forget the time when she's painting."

"You don't mind?"

"That my wife has something she loves to fill her days? Of course not. Besides, if she's occupied with her painting, that means she has less time to keep an eye on me," he winked.

Maggie playfully swatted Albert with a tea towel. "Oh you! For that you can clean up the dishes while Grace and I visit some more."

"Why should tonight be any different than any other night?" he chuckled.

Grace rose from the table. "Let me help. It's the least I can do to thank you for your hospitality. After the morning I've had, it's nice to spend time with someone friendly."

"Did something happen this morning?" Maggie wanted to know.

Grace realized her blunder when she saw their expectant faces.

"Leave her alone Mother. Maybe she doesn't want to talk about it."

"It's not that," Grace responded. "It's just that I have to get used to taking care of things on my own."

"Why would you want to do that when you have friends who want to help?" Maggie asked.

Grace glanced away for a moment, then she came to a decision. She told the couple about Mr. Franco's disparaging comments to herself and the young boys at the Trading Post.

Maggie sat back and sighed. "Oh dear, I would have thought that Henry would be over the fact that Sarah ran off with Joseph Swift."

"I don't understand."

"Most people around here accept the Natives as part of the community. Henry used to as well, until the woman he loved left town with another man. He never got over it. He's hated the Native people ever since."

Grace's brow furrowed in her attempt to follow.

"Sorry, I'm not making myself clear. About forty years ago, Henry Franco and Sarah Crow, as she was known then, fell in love. But her parents wouldn't let them get married because Henry is white."

"Do you mean to say that Sarah wasn't?" Grace had heard of such marriages, but she'd never met anyone who'd done it.

"That's right. Sarah's ancestors have lived in this area for generations, and they've been treated poorly by the whites.

Is it any wonder that they didn't want Sarah to marry outside their race?"

"So, if Henry Franco loved Sarah, who was a Native woman, why was he so mean to those young boys?" Grace inquired in an attempt to understand the workings of Mr. Franco's mind.

"I suppose it's his way of getting back at them for not thinking he was good enough for one of their own."

"So where is Sarah now?" Grace wondered out loud.

"She's in Sudbury, last I heard." Maggie said. "Not long after she moved there, she had a baby boy. Henry was devastated when he found out. He's been hostile to the indigenous people ever since."

Grace couldn't help but feel sorry for him. "It's not easy to lose someone you love."

"Didn't Sarah's family once own the camp where Grace is staying?" Albert asked.

"It's been some years," Maggie responded.

"Oh, that explains a lot," Grace said thoughtfully.

Now it was Maggie's turn to look puzzled. "I'm afraid I don't know what you're talking about."

"Well, when I mentioned to Mr. Franco where I was staying, he just shut right down."

"And you think it's because you're staying in Sarah's old cabin?"

"The thought does cross my mind," Grace said.

"Sarah's been gone for a long time now. Besides, Henry went on to marry Bertha. They had two daughters together," Maggie explained.

"So he's married?"

"He was until Bertha died a few years ago."

"And the girls?"

"They both married and moved away. I don't think he sees them much."

Grace helped Maggie to clear the table, while Albert washed the dishes. Grace hated to leave the company of her new friends. But it was getting late, and she still had to walk back through the unfamiliar woods.

Albert kindly offered to accompany her, but she declined. She needed some time to think. Upon saying goodnight, Maggie pulled her close and gave her a big hug. Albert, on the other hand, was a little more reserved and simply nodded his farewell.

IV

What seemed welcoming and cool during the day, was at night, cold and inhospitable. In fact, the night shadows along the path made it difficult for Grace to find her way back to her camp. Why hadn't she accepted Albert's offer of an escort? Eyes wide, she kept alert for any familiar markers that would guide her way home.

A loud shriek rent the night. "What was that?" she said aloud, as though she expected an answer. The sound came again from somewhere above her. Eyes heavenward, she searched through twilight branches brushed with red and gold and spied an owl staring down at her with large all-knowing eyes. Then something furry skittered across her feet. She squealed. The owl swooped down, snatched the unknown creature between its claws, and flew off into the night.

Grace was really frightened now. But in her haste to get back to camp, she didn't see the broken tree branch hidden beneath some pine needles. She pitched forward and landed on all fours with a jolt of pain. She scrambled to her feet and scurried along, while the earth moved at a dizzying pace beneath her, and the trees whispered an eerie cadence. What on earth she was doing out here?

A wave of relief washed over her when the river came into view, signaling that her camp was close at hand. In contrast to the dark woods, the river painted a picture of serenity. Moonlight glistened down upon the waters and created a feeling of safety. Almost there.

Just as her camp came into her field of vision, she heard a melodious rhythm dance on the night air. At first, she thought her senses were playing a trick on her. She searched the night, but there was no one there. How could it be? With a piercing glance from side to side, she began to run across the uneven ground. She couldn't think about what would happen if she fell. She had to get home. When her feet hit the steps of the deck, she stumbled to the top. She fumbled with the key to the door, while her eyes searched the night. It seemed an eternity before the lock gave way. When it did, she scurried inside, slammed the door, and locked it with a satisfying click.

She pressed her ear against the panels and held her breath. The silence dared her to peek out of the window beside the door. Everything appeared to be peaceful, and yet she knew she had heard something.

She stood frozen as the minutes passed. When no sound came forth to corroborate what her ears had surely heard, she moved away from the door. Afraid to go to bed, she sat in the beat-up old armchair in front of the window. The imperturbable scene before her seemed at odds with the strange occurrence. But she knew what she had heard. There was no longer any need for pretext. The singing she heard tonight was the same as what she'd heard on the night of the storm.

* * * * * *

Grace fell asleep in the chair that night. Consequently, she woke up the next morning feeling stiff.

In the light of day, the ghostly singing of the night before seemed far-fetched. There must be some simple explanation for what she heard; like maybe campers were singing around the campfire. Sound does travel well over water, after all. That certainly sounded more reasonable than some otherworldly occurrence brought on by too much excitement.

A loud knock startled Grace out of her musings.

"Yoo-hoo, is anybody home?" Maggie called out.

Grace sighed and opened the door. "What are you doing up and about so early in the morning?"

"Early!" Maggie piped. "I've been up with the birds. Don't want to waste a moment of this glorious day."

"Have you got time for a cup of coffee? I just put the pot on."

"Sounds good to me." Maggie followed Grace into the kitchen, where she made herself comfortable in one of the chairs.

"Have you had breakfast?"

"Ages ago. Just coffee for me."

Grace prepared toast for herself, and poured two cups of coffee, before settling down to eat.

"Albert and I were worried about you walking home last night. Obviously you got back in one piece."

"I don't mind saying that I was a little scared. I'm not used to the night sounds around here. It was a bit creepy."

"Best to have a flash light when you're out at night," Maggie said.

"I'll keep that in mind next time."

"It can't hurt to have a whistle as well, so you can call for help."

Grace nodded in agreement, but Maggie's comment made her realize how isolated things were out here.

"Four Mile island is relatively safe, but you never know. The residents change from time to time."

"Do you know how many camps there are on the island?"

"Well, let me see. Out of eleven, maybe five are occupied right now. We usually get more people in July and August. Then there are the occasional campers on the bay. That's pretty much it."

"Do you happen to know if anyone is camping right now?"

"I'm not sure. Why do you ask?"

"Well, I heard singing last night. I figured it must have come from some camp nearby."

"That's quite possible," Maggie nodded. "Say, why don't you come and keep me company today while I paint? It would give you a chance to explore a little bit."

Grace was relieved by Maggie's easy manner. "I'd love to keep you company."

"Perhaps you'd even like to try your hand at painting again?"

"Thanks, but I think I'd rather bring my journal."

"Now that we have that settled, we'd better get started. Don't bother to pack a lunch. Albert packed enough to feed a whole gang of people."

"Surely you exaggerate."

"Wait 'til you see. Albert's used to feeding a crowd. There's always people dropping in back home. He still hasn't adjusted to camp life yet."

"Really. Sounds rather carefree."

"I come from a large family. Someone is always dropping in unannounced. Or, could be I just told him to pack extra," Maggie said with a twinkle in her eye.

"Then, I'd better say yes, hadn't I?"

"Damn right you'd better," Maggie laughed.

They found a lovely spot to set up Maggie's easel by the bay, so she could paint wildflowers. Meanwhile, Grace found a log to sit on not far away and began to write in her journal.

Dear Charles: May 12, 1963

I'm sitting on the banks of the French River as I write this. You remember I once told you that my family came her often when I was a child? Well, I found this journal in the book case and started to read it. When I realized the entries were about a young couple who spent time on the island, I started to feel sorry for myself. Then I got this great idea to write to you, so I wouldn't feel so lonely.

Yesterday, I met a lovely couple while exploring the island. Maggie's an artist and is painting a landscape nearby, and her husband, Albert, is a horticulturist. They were kind enough to invite me to dinner last night. I had such a good time with them.

Maggie is like no other woman I've ever met before. She wears men's pants, would prefer to paint than cook, and wanders off on her own all the time. And the amazing thing is, her husband doesn't seem to mind. I wish I'd known her years ago.

My mother would be shocked that any woman would want to do anything other than take care of her family. She drummed it into my head that family comes first. I agree with her up to a point, but it would have been lovely to have something of my own.

It seems my entire married life was devoted to you and the children. We married right after you graduated from university. Remember? I quit half way through my English degree to help pay the bills, so you could get your PhD in History. Don't get me wrong, I was glad to help. I just wish I'd gone back to get my degree, after you were done, like we planned. But there wasn't time after the children came.

I tried to keep up by reading, and sometimes I wrote a little poetry, as you know. I even began that book club so I could spend time with adults and share my love of literature. It helped to fill the void, but I still felt guilty, because I wasn't satisfied with all that I had. There was just this part of me that wanted more.

I wish you could have understood when I told you I wanted to finish my degree after the kids went to school. But you were worried that they would get into trouble if there was no one to supervise them when they got home. I know you took great of pride in being able to support the family on your salary, so I let it go.

Well you're gone now, and I have nothing to fall back on. I regret that I didn't push for change. But times were different then, weren't they? I was different. I would never have dreamed of going against your wishes. It just wasn't done. So I tried to fill my days with other things. I tried to be happy, but sometimes there'd be this little space inside me that needed to be filled.

I don't tell you this to make you feel bad. I just want you to know how I felt all those years. I don't regret our time

*together. But you're gone now, and I have to figure out who
I am without you. I don't know if I'll like that person, or not,
but I have to try.*

Your loving wife,
Grace.

"Do you smell anything?" Maggie asked when Grace
closed her journal.

Grace sniffed the air. "It smells like fish frying over
a fire, and it seems to be coming from over there." She
pointed toward a break in the trees.

"Why don't we go and see who it is?" Maggie suggested.

"Should we disturb them?"

"It's always a good idea to find out who we're sharing the
island with."

"Have you ever had any problems?"

"Not often, but it doesn't hurt to be careful."

The two women packed up their gear and stepped
through a break in the trees. They didn't have far to go.
They soon came across a camp of four teenage boys, who
looked to be around sixteen or seventeen, sitting around a
campfire enjoying their catch.

"Hello the camp," Maggie called out.

The boys were cautious of the strangers in their midst.
The eldest one put his plate aside, wiped his mouth on the
back of his hand, and walked toward them. The mistrust in

his eyes changed, to one of recognition, when he realized who they were.

"James Whitefeather! What are you doing out here? And who is that you have with you?" Maggie looked past the young man to check out his companions.

Grace immediately recognized the boys from the Trading Post.

"Is this a friend of yours?" James inquired of Maggie.

"We only met yesterday, but yes, I consider her my friend. This is Grace Irwin," she said.

James stepped aside. "Do you want some coffee? There's plenty."

"Sounds good to me," Maggie said. "I'd never turn down a chance to visit."

James introduced his brother, Will, and their friends, Oscar and Leroy.

James served the coffee black, not bothering to offer what they apparently didn't have, and sat down to finish his meal.

"This is such a nice surprise. I never expected to see you all again," Grace said.

"Perhaps it would have been better if you hadn't," James said softly.

Grace was shocked. "Why do you say that?"

"You heard old man Franco. We Indians are all a bunch of thieves and not to be trusted."

"And is that true?"

"According to Franco, it is."

"You seem determined to have me think ill of you."

James shrugged.

"So, where are you boys headed?" Maggie redirected the conversation.

"As far as Hartley Bay," Will responded.

"How long will that take you?" Grace inquired.

"As long as is needed," James said matter-of-factly.

"I'm told the waters can be quite treacherous in some areas," Grace said.

"True enough," James agreed. "But we've lived on these waters our whole lives. We know what we're doing."

"Even so, as a parent, I'd be concerned."

"Life is full of danger."

"You have a point there," Grace said, thinking of how her own husband had died. "I guess we never know when our time is up."

"Only the Great Spirit knows that," James agreed.

"So, how long have you boys been here?" Maggie asked.

"We got in last night."

"Last night?" Grace began to wonder if it was the boys she heard singing last night. She covered up her surprise by adding, "Do you plan on staying long?"

"As long as we feel like it. The only thing that's certain is the destination."

Grace liked his thinking. "Well, I guess we should be going." Grace finished the rest of her coffee. "It certainly was nice seeing all of you again."

"Why don't you all come for supper tonight?" Maggie suggested.

Grace watched James glance at his companions who shrugged and nodded their agreement.

"Sounds good," James answered for them all.

"You know where I live. Come at six."

"We'll be there."

Grace offered to bring dessert. In fact she was looking forward to cooking for others again.

* * * * * *

The dinner was a simple affair of beef stew and biscuits, followed by Grace's chocolate cake.

"I understand you're on your way to Hartley Bay," Albert said.

"That's the plan," Will answered.

"That means you'll have to get past Recollet Falls. That's a pretty dangerous part of the river. Best to be careful."

"No worries there," Oscar bragged. "We know the river pretty well."

"I've heard of Recollet Falls," Grace interjected.

"It was named after six Recollet friars who died there in 1600's," Albert informed her. "That part of the river is rocky, and the water runs pretty swiftly. It can be quite dangerous if you don't know what you're doing. It's best to portage around it."

"We will," Leroy smiled.

"I envy you this adventure," Grace said. "I haven't been canoeing since I was a young girl, but I do remember enjoying it very well." It occurred to her that she had left the adventurous part of herself back in her childhood.

"Well then, why don't you let us take you for a little ride?" James offered.

"I couldn't possibly," Grace said. But a big part of her was thrilled at the prospect. Here was the chance she'd been waiting for. She shouldn't pass it up. But manners, drummed into her by her mother, dictated she not overstep the bounds of propriety. "This is your trip, and I don't want to intrude. Besides, I'd be really nervous in the swifts, or on the rapids for that matter." There it was. Fear. She wanted to do this, but she was afraid.

"We can take you around the island instead. There's no fast moving water there at all, so it will be safe."

"Really?" She grinned from ear to ear. "All right."

There was a round of cheers that left Grace blushing. The boys invited Maggie and Albert to join them, but they graciously declined.

When Grace got home later that evening, she was too excited to sleep, so she grabbed her journal and began to write.

Dear Charles: May 12, 1963 - Evening

While Maggie and I were out today, we ran into the four young boys I met at the Trading Post camped by the bay.

They've pitched their tents on one of several flat areas that didn't look terribly comfortable for sleeping. But I imagine they weren't bothered. They are young, after all, and care little for the base comforts that we grown-ups become used to. They were just finishing a hot lunch when we arrived.

After a cautious introduction, they invited us to their campfire for coffee. They plan to canoe as far as Hartley Bay which will take them a few days. I am amazed at the confidence of ones so young. The waters of the French can be so unpredictable. I have never felt that sure of myself in my entire life.

Being with them reminds me of our own boys, so I was glad that Maggie offered the dinner invitation. It was an opportunity to get to know them better. And if I was completely honest with myself, I wanted to find out why Henry Franco made such a big fuss about their character. The truth is, I found them to be well-mannered, intelligent young men and no different from our own boys.

The evening went well. Albert made a wonderful stew, and my chocolate cake was a great success.

It turns out that Albert and James have a lot in common. They are both interested in the land, so they talked a great deal about the flora of the area. Will was obviously proud of his big brother, but there was also a competitive streak in him that wants to challenge James, especially when James tries to tell him what to do. Oscar is the shortest member of the group and has a friendly personality. Leroy, a heavy-set young man, was content to sit back and let others have the limelight. He is easy going and quick to laugh, but I sensed a deeper maturity that he keeps hidden.

The evening reminded me so much of our own family time. Remember how we used to sit around the dinner table and talk about our day? It was strangely comforting, but it left me feeling sad at the same time.

The boys have offered to take me canoeing tomorrow. I can hardly wait. It's been such a long time since I've been out in a canoe. I hope I still remember how it's done.

I never realized how much I've missed this kind of life. I've always enjoyed being close to nature. It fills me with a sense of peace I haven't known in a long time. The people I've met are so different from the ones back home. They're people of the earth: grounded and self-possessed.

I'd better get to sleep. They'll be here early in the morning.

Good night my love,
Grace

V

As promised, the boys arrived early to take Grace on their canoe trip around the island. James and Will held on to the dock with one hand, so Grace was able to slide down into the bobbing craft. She remembered to stay low and centered, so the boat wouldn't capsize. Leroy and Oscar waited patiently in the other canoe. Once they were all situated, the boys dipped their paddles into the water and, using a side slip stroke, pulled away from the dock.

When they set off, the morning was cool and overcast after an overnight rain. But it promised to warm up as the day wore on.

The boys initially did all the paddling while Grace sat back and let the breeze, created by the momentum of the canoe, wash over her face. It gave her a chance to focus her attention on the surrounding landscape, which was wild and rustic, just as God made it.

The land was on high ground, so they were surrounded by rocks and trees on both sides: Four Mile Island on one side and Eighteen Mile Island on the other. It felt like they were the only people who existed in the world. After a while,

Grace wanted to see if she remembered how to paddle. Will was happy to let her take over. Though her initial technique was a little clumsy, with a little coaching from Will, it soon came back to her.

After a while, Grace's muscles began to ache, so she switched sides. The light canoe moved swiftly along the river. Though it was a little tiring for someone who wasn't used to it, Grace found canoeing quite exhilarating.

The waters of the French were teeming with bass, pike, walleye and Muskie, so they stopped at lunch time to see what they could catch. Grace helped to unload the canoes, and they set up camp. While she collected wood for a fire, the boys found a fishing spot. It didn't take long before they had enough fish for lunch.

Grace had fond memories of watching her father gut fish when she was a little girl, but only from a distance. It was something that both fascinated and disgusted her. She stepped up behind Leroy to watch the process over his shoulder. He had already scaled the bass and was about to cut into it. She gulped.

"Want to give it a try?" Leroy asked when he was done the first fish.

"Me, gut a fish?" She stumbled backwards, and her hands flailed about.

"Why not you?" Leroy handed her the knife.

Grace looked from the knife, to the fish, and then to Leroy's round chubby face with the perpetual smile. "I'm afraid I've never done this before," she admitted, sheepishly.

"I figured that." He grabbed another fish and slapped it on the flat rock. He pulled her forward, placed the knife in her hand, and guided it from tail to head. "Start by making a slit along the belly," he said.

"Right here?"

"That's right. Now press the tip of the knife in and slice along here." He pointed once again to the underside of the fish.

Grace could feel the pull of meat and muscle as she sliced.

"Good. Now open her up, and pull out the guts."

Grace gingerly slid her fingers inside the fish and felt around. She screwed up her face at the first contact with the unfamiliar guts.

"You've got to pull the skin apart like this," Leroy instructed. "You want to get your hands right in there. That's better."

Grace watched in horror, as blood and guts spilled out onto the rock. Leroy scooped it up and tossed it into the river. Bait for other fish, Grace supposed.

"Now rinse it."

Grace complied. She was more than happy to wash the guts off her hands at the same time. When Leroy was satisfied she'd done a good job, he said, "Now you have to cut off the fins."

She sawed at the fins until they came off.

"Now, all that's left is the head."

Grace swiped an arm across her brow.

"Place the knife under the gills right here and slice." He indicated a spot below where the eyes stared back at her.

She searched for the right spot with her fingers. "Here?" she said.

"That's it. Now slide the knife all the way through, and you're done."

Grace held the fish firmly in one hand while she made the cut. The head went into the river along with the guts.

"Want to try another one?" Leroy asked.

"I think I get the idea," Grace demurred.

Grace couldn't bear to eat any fish she'd just gutted, so she settled for the cheese sandwiches she'd made for lunch.

After a morning of unaccustomed exercise, Grace fell asleep under a languid afternoon sun. When she woke up, James was reading, and Leroy was gazing up at the sky.

"Where are Will and Oscar?" she asked.

"Can't you hear them?" James said.

She got up, followed the sound of their laughter, and found them diving off the rocks into the crystal clear water. They egged each other on to do something more daring: somersaults, back flips, twists, and turns. Grace sat down to watch and marvelled at their skill and daring.

James sat down beside her. "Why don't you join them?"

"The water's too cold for me," she said. "I'll just watch. What about you?"

"I've already been for a swim."

"I hope my little nap didn't hold you up?"

"We're in no hurry."

"Are you always like this?"

"Like what?"

"So calm."

"I've never really thought about it."

"Yesterday you didn't seem the least bit concerned about how long it will take you to get to Hartley Bay, and today you're in no hurry to canoe around the island. Most young people want everything right away."

"What's the rush? There's nowhere else I need to be," he shrugged. "Except in this moment."

"I can't imagine why you'd want to spend any of your time with someone who is old enough to be your mother."

He grinned. "And I can't imagine why you'd want to spend an afternoon with a bunch of noisy teenagers."

"Maybe because there are times when I miss my own sons," she countered.

"How many do you have?"

"Two, but they have their own hopes and dreams, and I have mine."

"What are yours?" James asked.

Grace frowned. "What?"

"You said you have your own hopes and dreams. What are they?"

She sat back and shrugged. "Did I actually say that?"

"Afraid so."

Grace blushed, and stared off into the distance, oblivious to the continued antics of Will and Oscar. She bit her nails. "It's been a long time since anyone has asked me what my dreams are. I thought I knew once, but I'm not sure any more. Once upon a time I wanted to teach."

"What happened?"

Grace shrugged. "I got married."

"It's not too late."

"That time has passed for me. I'm not the same person I was then."

James nodded. His book dangled from his hand between his spread legs. "Maybe it's time to start thinking about what you'd like to do now," he suggested.

"Mmmm. You're probably right. And what about you? What are your dreams?"

"That's part of what this trip is about; to figure out what to do next."

"Any thoughts?"

"I'll probably do what my father did and work as a guide."

"Is that what you want?"

"I like working on the land, so it seems like a good fit."

"Yes, I can see that you love this landscape." She surveyed their rugged surroundings.

James chuckled. "Is it that obvious?"

"I'm afraid so," she said. "Can you make a good living being a guide?"

"My father managed. Besides, I'd like to stick around. My mother doesn't complain, but I know life's been hard for her since my father left. Now that I'm old enough to work full time, I can help out," he explained.

"Do you mind my asking what happened to your father?"

James shrugged. "It's no big secret. He was in the war, saw too much killing, and just wasn't the same after. He never did adjust to civilian life again. He decided it would be better for everyone if he just left. So my mom had to take care of Will and me by herself. Now that I'm old enough to get a job, maybe things will be easier for her."

"How old were you when he left."

"Twelve."

Grace thought about her own situation. Charles had been stationed at Camp Petawawa training base during the war, and therefore, far from any action. At least he came home whole. "I'm so sorry to hear that. It must have been hard growing up without a father."

"We managed."

"So now you've decided to fill in for your father," she guessed.

He shrugged.

"So what about you? Who takes care of you?"

"We take care of each other."

"What about your dreams?" Grace waited for his response.

"I have no illusions. Even though I finished High School, there's not much in the way of opportunities for my kind. Besides, I don't have to do anything to be somebody."

"I've only read about the residential schools in the history books," Grace said.

"I didn't go to a residential school."

"Oh. I thought all Native children had to go residential school."

"Some still do. But we had our own school on the Dokis Reserve," he said.

"I'm glad," was all she could think to say.

* * * * * *

On their way back to camp, Grace learned that many of the cabins along the river had no electricity, telephones, or indoor plumbing. There was, however, an outhouse dug away from the cabin. Fortunately, that had all changed where she was staying. She could boast both electricity and plumbing.

"Look, a cormorant," Will called out from the other canoe.

James and Grace soon caught sight of the huge black bird as they rounded the next bend. Its webbed feet were wrapped around a tree branch weighing it down. They brought the canoes to a standstill, with a reverse forward stroke of the paddle, but the yellow-beaked bird saw them and flew away.

Between the sun and the unfamiliar exercise, Grace was exhausted by the time Crow's Nest came into view. James and Will propelled the canoe up alongside the dock. James climbed out to help Grace gain her footing, as the dock dipped and swayed. Once she felt comfortable on dry land again, she said, "I want to thank you for taking me out in your canoe today. I had a lovely time."

There followed a chorus of, "You're welcome." "No problem." And, "You bet."

"You make sure you come back and see me when your canoe trip is over. I want to hear all about it," Grace said before she let them go.

"Sure," James said, as he passed her tucker up to her. Then, with an expert turn of their canoes, they paddled out of sight.

Grace felt a deep loneliness, as she watched them drift further away. Once they were out of sight, she picked up the remains of her picnic lunch and headed indoors. Her legs and arms were stiff from hours spent paddling in a crouched position in the bottom of a canoe. A hot shower and bed were definitely in her future.

After a hot meal, Grace curled up in her usual place by the window and opened her journal.

Dear Charles: May 13, 1963

I'm really missing you tonight. The emptiness of my days weighs heavily on me sometimes. This, despite the fact that I just spent a lovely day canoeing around Four Mile Island with the new friends I told you about. But they're gone now, and I feel rather lost without their company.

I do so admire these young boys. They exhibit such an adventurous spirit much like the voyageurs of old. They too, will have to face the potentially dangerous waters of the French. I wish I had the same calm fearlessness they do. Maybe someday. My corner of the world has always been so safe and predictable. And to be fair to you, that's what I wanted. But now I see that another kind of life is possible.

When James asked me what my dreams are, I seem to recall wanting to be a teacher. But it's too late for that now. I could always write. But who am I kidding? It takes years to master that particular craft. I think I'd like to be more like Maggie. She certainly seems to enjoy a life of her own making. She paints, while her husband cooks. I still can't get over that.

James doesn't seem to feel he has much of a future. Being Native, he has no illusions about his prospects. Life has already been hard on him. His father came back from the war damaged and unable to assimilate. Interesting that I should pick that particular word. It personifies what happened to his people. They were forced to assimilate to the white man's way of life by French Missionaries in the 1600s. And if that wasn't enough, the Canadian government took children away from their families and put them into residential schools. Thank God James was saved from that fate. Others weren't so lucky, I know. They were stripped of their culture and way of life. Many of the children died from poor treatment and were isolated from their loved ones. It breaks my heart to think of it. But you know all this, don't you?

I guess in retrospect, I have a lot to be grateful for. Why isn't it enough?

Grace.

On impulse, Grace grabbed her terry robe off the bed and headed for the door. She really was feeling sorry for herself tonight. Maybe the swaying motion of the hammock would relax her. She was just getting comfortable when she heard it – the singing. She quickly swung her legs back around so her feet hit the ground and prepared for flight. Her eyes scanned the river and tree line, but she couldn't see anything that would warrant the sudden pounding in her chest.

To be on the safe side, Grace hurried back inside and locked the door, secured the windows, and once again kept a lookout in the chair by the window. Then she chided herself. The boys were on the island the first time she heard the singing. And they were still on the island – at least for one more night. Could it be them singing songs around the camp fire? If that was the case, she was being ridiculous sitting here keeping watch like this. She went to bed.

VI

Being married to a history professor had, over the years, encouraged Grace's own curiosity about the places she visited in her travels. She knew the French River was once a pathway to the West, but she wanted to know more. So she decided to stop in town to find out where she could learn more about the history of the area. Maybe someone at the diner would know who she could talk to. When she walked in, people stared. But there was no turning back now. She walked past the booths toward to counter, where she sat on one of the red padded stools bolted to the floor.

"What'll you have?" the uniformed waitress asked. She slapped the menu in front of Grace and poured coffee into a white mug.

"Just some coffee and maybe some information."

"Okay, shoot," the waitress said and leaned her plump frame on the counter.

"Do you happen know where I could find out about the history of the area?" Grace asked.

"You'd be wanting to speak to George Watson. Hey George," she yelled across the diner to a booth by the window. "There's a lady here who wants to use the library. When are you opening up shop?"

George Watson squinted over the top of his dark-rimmed glasses and said, "As soon as I'm done my breakfast."

Mr. Watson was wearing a white shirt that strained at the buttons over his stomach. He sported a thin comb-over a balding pate, and he seemed in no hurry to leave, despite the fact that he knew she was waiting for him. She had to remind herself that people in this part of the country followed a different rhythm than what she was used to in the city.

"Please take your time," Grace assured him. "I'm in no hurry."

While Grace waited for Mr. Watson to finish his breakfast, she took the time to look around the establishment. Though slightly run-down, the diner was spotless, and the coffee was delicious. Whoever owned this place certainly did a brisk business. The reason became quickly evident while she watched the waitress chat with the customers.

Grace picked up the menu to keep herself occupied, while she drank her coffee. She barely had time to start reading, before the friendly waitress came back to top up her cup.

"You're new around here aren't you?" she asked.

"That's right, my name's Grace Irwin." She held out her hand.

"Glad to meet you." The woman shook Grace's hand. "Mary Whitefeather. I run this place."

"Did you say, Whitefeather?" Grace asked.

"Sure did."

"As in related to James and Will Whitefeather?"

"What have they done now? I knew I should never have let them go on that canoe trip. What was I thinking?"

Grace laughed. "No, no, they haven't done anything wrong."

A bell rang, followed by a call from the kitchen, that an order was ready. "Don't go anywhere." Mary retrieved her order at a window situated between the kitchen and dining area.

"Betty could you cover for me while I find out what my boys have been up to?" Mary said upon her return.

"Sure thing," the other waitress called back.

Mary parked herself next to Grace. "So tell me how you know my boys?"

"Maggie Williams introduced us while they were camped at Four Mile Island. I'm staying at Crow's Nest there. After we chatted for a while, Maggie invited us all over for dinner. My, they do like to eat don't they?"

"Tell me about it. I have a hard time keeping food in the house."

"Well, they certainly cleaned up that night. It reminded me of when my own two boys were still living at home. They didn't waste food either. Anyway, to make a long story short, they offered to take me on a canoe ride around the island the following day, yesterday, that is, and I accepted. I had a wonderful time."

"So, they're gone now?"

"Yes, as far as I know, they left this morning."

"Well, it's good to know they're all right. Being a single parent is tough sometimes. You worry."

"Yes, it does take some getting used to," Grace agreed.

"So, you're on your own?" Mary guessed.

"Yes," Grace answered.

"Well at least you don't have to watch out for your boys anymore."

"I wish that were true, but I don't think you ever really stop worrying about them."

"You mean it never ends?" Mary teased.

"I'm afraid not," Grace laughed.

"Well I'd better get back to work before the boss fires me," Mary joked. "But you come back again real soon, ya hear?"

"As long as you keep serving up this delicious coffee, you can count on seeing me quite often. It's a whole lot better than what I make."

"How do you think I stay in business?"

While Grace finished her coffee, she realized that Mr. Watson had left while she'd been busy talking to Mary. It was time for her to go as well.

* * * * * *

She secured directions from Mary and found Mr. Watson's place a few doors down from the diner. It was a single-level dwelling, rustic in design, with a sign out front that good-naturedly proclaimed that she was in the right place.

She walked up the front four steps and opened the door. Mr. Watson was already sitting behind his desk hard at work. The library itself was smaller than outward appearances would assume. She surmised that perhaps Mr. Watson lived in the back part of the building. He looked up when she presented herself before him.

"Grace Irwin." She reached out a hand to him. "We sort of met at the diner a few minutes ago. I passed the time having a coffee, while I waited for you to open the library."

"Of course. What can I do for you?"

"I'm looking for a history book about the area. Do you have anything?"

"Can you be more specific?"

"Well, I know that the French River was a fur trading route at one time. I'd like to learn all about that."

"I can tell you all about that." He offered her a place to sit beside him.

"Um, well," Grace sputtered. "I don't want to be a bother. I was hoping to simply sign out a book and read all about it myself."

"The history of the area is a passion of mine. I'd be more than happy to tell you all I know. I've been keeping a record for years."

Grace took note that they were the only two people in the library. She wondered if there was a wife in the picture. Her mind went back to Toronto, and the threat she had become to the husbands of her friends. According to them, she was now a widowed woman and supposedly on the look-out for male companionship. She didn't want to get into that kind of situation again. She decided however, that since they were technically in a public place, no one could possibly think that anything untoward was going on, so she said, "I suppose it would be all right."

"You know I don't get that many people in here asking about the history of the area," he said once she was settled.

"That surprises me. I would have thought that a lot of people would be interested in the local history."

"Tourists mostly, but they're few and far between. They're more interested in the fishing and hunting. As for the locals, they already know about the area. They've been passing down oral stories for generations. That's where I get a lot of my information, which I cross reference with journals and history books where I can."

"Why do you study it if no one's going to read it?"

"Someone has to keep a record for future generations. Besides, I enjoy doing it. It helps to pass the time, while my wife is visiting our daughter in Sudbury."

So he was married. "You must miss her?" she offered.

"Yes, well," he mumbled. "Shall we get started?"

Grace got out her writing pad and pen to take notes.

"As you already know, the French River was a fur trading route for the French voyageurs in the early 1600s."

"Is that how the river got its name?" Grace asked. "Because the French were the first Europeans to travel its waterways?"

"You're right about that. But what you might not know is, the Ojibwe called the river Wemitigoozhe Ziibii. Wemitigoozhe means Stick-Waver, and Ziibii means River. As the story goes, when the Jesuit missionaries brought Christianity to the tribes, they'd wave two sticks tied together in the shape of a cross. This was a symbol of their vocation, you see. But the Natives thought it amusing and started to call them Wemitigoozhe, or Stick-Wavers. After that, all the French people who came to the area were considered Stick-Wavers."

While Grace took notes, George went on to tell her how the Natives have been using the French River for trade long before the white man turned up. He filled her in on how Samuel de Champlain sent Étienne Brûlé to live with the Huron in order to improve trade relations with the Natives. Then he turned around to rebuke Brûlé for adopting the ways of the Huron. He spoke of how the voyageurs traded beaver, from Montreal to Lake Athabasca, covering 3,000 miles of waterways.

But when he said, "You know there's a legend around here that says, if you listen carefully, you can still hear the voices of the voyageurs singing as they paddle their canoes across the water," Grace's heart started to thump in her chest.

"Is something wrong?" George asked, noting her flushed face.

Before she could answer, someone entered the library. George went over to see if he could be of assistance.

"I'm sorry about that," George said upon his return. "Are you all right now?"

"I'm fine. Now, what was that you were you saying about the voyageurs?"

"Oh yes, I've heard tales of people who have heard the voyageurs singing."

"Do you believe it's true?"

He shrugged. "You hear all kinds of stories like that around here. People tend to romanticize the history to interest the tourists."

"So you don't believe it?"

"Like I said, it makes a good story for the tourists."

"I suppose so," Grace said absentmindedly.

"Well, we've been at this for some time now. You must be tired of listening to me ramble on."

"On the contrary, I've enjoyed it. But perhaps it is time for me to go."

"Of course," he said.

Grace had to work hard to stay focused, as she eased her motor boat away from the dock. Especially when she reached the swifts. She couldn't afford to damage the boat on any hidden rocks. Once safely through, she sped up and headed for home.

All that afternoon, thoughts kept jumping around in her head. OK, suppose she did hear singing? Was it really the voyageurs like in the legend? Why was she the one to hear it? And what could it possibly mean? Maybe writing in her journal would ease her restless thoughts.

Dear Charles: May 14, 1963

I just had the most unsettling conversation. I went to visit the local librarian, George Watson, to learn more about the history of the French River. And what he told me was quite startling. Apparently, there's a local myth that people have actually heard the voyageurs singing. I almost fell off my chair. Can you believe it? He doesn't believe the myth himself. He says that it brings the tourists to the area.

I don't know if I feel better, knowing that other people have heard the singing as well, or not. If it is for real, then something otherworldly is going on here. That's an unsettling thought. At least it means I'm not completely crazy.

I wish you were here right now to hold me, and tell me everything will be OK. You always were steadying force in our relationship. I know you're familiar with mythological phenomenon through your studies. I suppose this could be considered the same type of thing — a story associated with a particular group or event in history. I also know that these stories are sometimes made up, like Mr. Watson says. But how could it be made up if I've heard it with my own ears? Is it really possible to hear singing from long-dead voyageurs? There must be something to it, but what?

I've been thinking, I'd like to write a memoir of my time at the French. Should I include the mysterious singing? Would people find it fascinating, or think I'm crazy? Sometimes I wonder if I've allowed others to guide my thinking too much. Maybe it's because I'm afraid to make a mistake. But what have I missed out on by playing it safe? Would anyone be interested in reading the memoir of a woman like me? Anyway, I do enjoy writing about it. Even if it means the only people who will read it are the boys. At least they'll have something to remember me by when I'm gone.

Your loving wife,
Grace.

VII

The following day, Grace decided to do some spring-cleaning. She'd been in no shape to do anything when she first arrived at camp, but now she felt ready to put things in order. It didn't take long to realize that no one had done anything, beyond tidying up, for a long time. It was no wonder then, that she was covered in dust when Mary Whitefeather paid a visit late in the day.

"Is anybody home?" Mary called out through the screen door.

"Well, this certainly is a surprise. To what do I owe the pleasure?"

Mary held up a basket and said, "I brought you some oatmeal muffins from the diner."

"Oh my, how lovely." She accepted the basket and it took into the kitchen followed closely by Mary.

"I usually bring vegetables, when I visit people along the river, but they're not ready yet."

"You grow vegetables?"

"Yeah. It's a way to make some extra cash during the summer."

"But you own the diner."

"So?"

"So where do you find the time to grow vegetables and sell them?"

"I can't take all the credit. The boys usually help. But until they get back from their canoe trip, I'll have to do it all myself. I don't mind. It's a change from being stuck inside the diner all the time. Besides, the summer is when I make most of my money, so I have to take advantage of it. Come winter, it's a lot harder."

Grace emptied the basket. "Wait, what's this?" She picked up a black bathing suit, from the bottom of the basket, and swung it around in her hand.

"Since it's such a nice spring day, I was hoping I could talk you into going for a swim in the bay?" Mary answered with a twinkle in her eyes.

"Won't the water be cold this time of year?"

"Probably, but that's not going to stop us, is it?"

Grace laughed. "Well, in that case I should probably pack a warm sweater for when we get out of the water," she mused aloud. "And what about some sandwiches for later?"

"Now you're getting into the spirit of things," Mary said.

* * * * * *

The water in the bay was cold, like Grace predicted, but they soon grew accustomed to it. It helped to keep moving in order to stay warm. They shivered when it was time to get out and dry off. And their clothes stuck to their damp bodies, as they struggled to dress.

"This is nice." Grace said. "I feel like I'm playing hooky."

"It's a treat for me too," Mary said. "Summer gets pretty busy."

"I can imagine," Grace said.

The two women surveyed a grouping of pine trees, across the bay, rooted firmly in the bedrock. Grace noted that the flat spot in the center would make an ideal campsite.

"I heard about your husband," Mary said after a while. "I'm sorry."

Grace's head snapped around to face Mary. "How did you..."

Mary shrugged. "I work in a diner. Word gets around."

Grace nodded. "Thank you. It was all rather sudden. He died of a heart attack."

"Do you have any other family? Besides your sons, I mean?"

"My parents are still living, but its best if I maintain a discreet distance from my mother. She doesn't think I can take care of myself."

"That sounds pretty normal."

"It's more than that. She wants to run my life. She always has."

"Well, everyone around here is related in one way or another. We're always messing about in each other's business," Mary responded.

"Doesn't that drive you crazy?"

"Only all the time."

"Then you know what I'm talking about."

"Mmmm." Mary lay back on a rock and gazed at the tree-tops, swaying in the breeze, and watched the clouds scud across the sky.

Grace surveyed the water in the bay which was so clear you could see right to the bottom. She shivered when a breeze skipped over her. She put on a heavy sweater, and wrapped it around her shoulders, for extra warmth.

Grace glanced at her friend for a moment, then turned away. Then, as if she had come to a decision, she twisted her body to look down at Mary, and said, "I know about your husband too. James told me."

Mary shrugged.

"It must have been difficult for you."

"It was probably for the best. David wasn't the same man I married when he came home from the war."

"So James said."

"At least he had the good sense to leave before it got too bad."

"You seem to have managed very well on your own. I don't know if I could have done as well in your position."

Mary sat up and stared pointedly at Grace. "In case you haven't noticed, you are in my position."

"But my children are all grown up, and I don't have to run a business by myself."

"You still have to pay the bills."

"Well, Charles had a life insurance policy, so the house is paid for."

"You seem all fire determined not to give yourself credit for anything," Mary pointed out.

Grace was taken aback by Mary's pronouncement. She looked around, as though she might pull the answer out of the air. "I don't know what to say."

"There are no measurements for what's hard, you know. Hard is hard. Just because your house is paid for and mine isn't, doesn't mean things are any easier for you than they are for me," Mary said.

"I never thought of myself as a strong person," Grace said in a quiet voice.

"Well, there's nothing like a little life lesson to find out," Mary said.

"But what if I fail?"

"Is that what you're afraid of?" Mary demanded.

"Aren't you?"

"Oh for Pete's sake," Mary admonished. "I don't have time to worry about such things. And you shouldn't either."

Grace had to reflect on this new perspective about herself. She wondered what would define a strong woman. She didn't have the answer, but it was certainly worth examining over the next little while.

"You're far away," Mary interrupted her musings.

"Just thinking about what you said."

"And?"

"Just that you make me think about things I've never considered before."

"Like what?"

"Once upon a time, I had plans."

"That so? What happened?"

"Got married," Grace replied.

"You're too young to be idle for the rest of your life."

"What if it's too late for me?"

"With that kind of thinking, it will be. Buck up, and start making plans for yourself."

"You don't pull any punches do you?"

"I don't have time to worry about what's proper. I have to keep a roof over our heads."

Grace loved that she could speak so openly with this woman. This kind of guileless talk was liberating. There's no fussing around with niceties. Just plain talk.

"Well, you've certainly done a wonderful job with your two boys," Grace said, changing the subject. "They're amazing. Especially James. He's so mature."

"With David gone, he's had to grow up quickly."

"Does your husband keep in touch?"

"He sends money when he can, and he usually remembers to send the boys a birthday card and a gift at Christmas."

"That's something anyway."

"I know, but it's tough to move on when you keep getting reminders that he's out there somewhere."

"At least the boys know that their father is thinking about them," Grace pointed out.

"Yeah, I guess you're right." Mary stood up then, and said, "Best get some firewood if we want tea."

While the water heated in the circle of stones left over from a previous fire, they sat back to enjoy a meal of salmon sandwiches and the muffins Mary brought from the diner.

"So, how are you making out on your own?" Mary asked.

"I wish I knew."

"There you go again not recognizing what you've accomplished. You're here aren't you? That's something."

"I suppose so. But that's about all I've done, I'm afraid."

"You've only been widowed a few months, yet you had the guts to come here on your own. Could be you're tougher than you think."

Grace sat up straight, and said, "I never thought of that."

"Come on, let's go skinny dipping," Mary said, lightening the mood.

"Are you nuts? Someone might see us."

"No-one's going to see us." Mary got up to remove her clothes, walked to the water's edge, and slipped into its shadowy depth.

Grace looked on with longing, then she came to a decision. She knew her mother would be appalled. Before she lost her nerve, she quickly undressed and followed Mary into the silky water. "Brrr, it's freezing," Grace said, bobbing up and down in the water, as she sculled beside Mary.

"We won't stay in long." The water gleamed on her face, and her dark hair was slick against her skull.

"You've done this before, haven't you?"

"Plenty of times," Mary said, knowingly. Their laughter caused them to lose their sculling rhythm, and they went under. They came up sputtering and shivering. It was time to get out.

They climbed onto the rocky ground, so they could dress. The fire had died down, so Mary added a fallen log, and they warmed up on hot tea.

"It's too bad we don't have something stronger to drink," Mary said. "We'll have to plan better next time."

"You know, I've never done anything like that before in my life," Grace admitted.

"You mean skinny dipping?"

"Yes. Although I used to come here with my family when I was a kid, my mother had very definite ideas about how a young lady should comport herself."

"I guess she wouldn't like me much then, would she?"

"You'd definitely be a challenge to her," Grace laughed. She leaned back on her elbows and stared up at the vast expanse of sky. "I don't think I'll ever get used to how bright the stars are around here," Grace said dreamily.

"It reminds me of a story my Grandfather used to tell me," Mary said.

"Will you share it with me?"

"It's the Anishinaabe story of Creation."

"Anishi-what?"

"Anishinaabe. It's the name given to our people. It means, Original Man. "As the story goes, Gitchie Manitou had a vision. From this vision he created the sky, sun, moon, stars, and earth as we know it, with all the plants, trees and animals. Then he created man by blowing into the sacred shell of earth, wind, fire, and water, and lowered him to earth on the back of a turtle. Then the floods came. The loon, beaver, and otter all dove into the water as far down as they could to bring up some dirt. But each one failed to reach the bottom. When the muskrat offered to swim to the bottom of the water, everyone laughed at him. 'You're too small. But go if you must.' He was gone so long that everyone thought he must have drowned. But the muskrat was fearless, and eventually his head popped up above the water, and in his paw was a clump of dirt. He placed this bit of earth onto the back of the turtle and it became known as, Turtle Island. Then Gitchie Manitou gave man a wolf to be his brother, and together they walked the earth to name the plants and animals."

Grace though on this for a moment before she responded. "What a lovely story. But what is this place called Turtle Island? I've never heard of it before."

"Why would you? It's the Anishinaabe name for North America. If you look at a map of North America, you'll see that the United States and Canada make up the body of the turtle, California and Florida are the legs, Mexico is the tail, and Alaska is the head."

Grace closed her eyes as she tried to picture it in her mind. "Oh yes, I see it now. The Anishinaabe story of creation is not so different from the Christian version, is it? They each speak of a creator who conjures the world as we know it."

"Interesting that," Mary said with a knowing smile. "I don't know about you, but I'm freezing my butt off here. We'd better get back to camp." She emptied the contents of the teapot onto the fire, then added some dirt, to make sure the fire was completely extinguished.

It was such a comfort for Grace to have someone to share her time with. She was especially grateful that she didn't have to find her way back to camp by herself. She'd remembered to bring a flash light this time, so they could find the way in the dark. When they arrived home, Grace invited Mary to stay the night.

"Sure, why not? There's no one waiting for me at home. But I'll have to get back bright and early. I have to open the diner first thing in the morning."

"That won't be a problem. I'm an early riser."

"Thanks for putting me up like this," Mary said while they made up the bed in the spare bedroom.

"It's no bother. It will be nice to have another human being close by again."

"Yeah, I know what you mean. I've missed having the boys around."

"Do you ever think about what you'll do when the boys are gone for good?" Grace asked.

"I'll go on as I always have."

"You don't want to get married again?"

"I'm already married. Besides, once was enough for me."

"Of course."

"What about you?" Mary wanted to know. "Do you think you'll ever marry again?"

"It's too soon for me to say. I miss Charles. In my heart I still feel married. To be with someone else would feel like a betrayal. You know what I mean?"

Mary nodded her understanding.

Grace loaned Mary a nightgown and showed her where the bathroom was.

"My turn," Grace said when Mary was done. "There's wine in the fridge if you're interested."

"Sounds good to me. I'll pour a glass for both of us."

"Is that popcorn I smell?" Grace said upon entering the kitchen a few minutes later.

"I hope you don't mind. I found it while I was looking for the glasses. I couldn't resist."

"I'm glad you made yourself at home."

While Mary got the popcorn ready, Grace went into the living room to start the fire that lay ready in the hearth. The two women were soon curled up on the old couch sharing their salty treat.

Mary took her first sip of wine. "This is good. I can't remember the last time I had a drink. The money I make has to go toward necessities. But I just know I'm going to regret this in the morning."

"The last time I did this, I was drowning my sorrows."

"Over your husband's death?"

"Well, sort of." Grace paused to collect her thoughts. "Did you ever think you knew your place in the scheme of things only to find out it was all a lie?"

"What do you mean?"

"When Charles died everyone was so kind to me. His colleagues took over some of the chores that belonged to Charles, and at first their wives brought food and sympathy. Honestly, I was grateful for the help. I never thought how it might look to others."

"Let me guess," Mary said. "The wives got jealous?"

Grace rubbed the spot between her eyes with quivering fingertips. "I don't know what I was thinking."

"That's the problem kid. You weren't thinking. How can you be expected to see anything clearly when your heart is broken?"

"I should have known..." Grace whispered through a lump in her throat.

"And so should they," Mary said vehemently. "Your friends should have known that you would never betray them."

"How can you know that?" Grace said with hope in her eyes. "You hardly know me."

"Look, you don't work in a diner for as long as I have without learning a thing or two about people."

"Oh." Grace replied.

"So who spilled the beans?" Mary asked bluntly.

"Spilled the beans?"

"Yes. Who told you that you were trespassing?"

"Well, it wasn't one person in particular. I accidentally overheard some of the wives while I was in the grocery store. I was just about to make my presence known when my name came up. And not in a good way." Grace sniffed and wiped her nose with the back of her hand. She watched Mary's face for her reaction. "It seems that, as a widow, I'm no longer welcome in their circle. I'm too much of a threat."

"And what do you think?" Mary challenged.

"They're wrong of course. I've just lost my husband. I can't imagine being with another man – and certainly not one of them."

"Whoo hoo! She's got some pluck in her after all."

"And do you know what else?" Grace said, warming up to her subject. "I've since discovered that these women are not my friends."

"That's more like it."

"Seriously, I really thought they were my friends. Yet when I needed them the most, they let me down."

"Not all of them, surely?"

"Maybe not. But, right now, I don't know who my friends are."

Mary squeezed Grace's hand and said, "I'll be your friend."

Grace placed her hand on top of Mary's and, with tears in her eyes, replied, "And I'll be yours."

Mary sat back in her chair. "So that's when you decided to get drunk."

Grace chuckled. "I'm afraid so. I paid for it the next day, though."

"With coffee and regrets," Mary said.

"How did you know?"

"Finding out the truth about your life always comes with regrets," she answered. "So is that when you decided to get out of town for a while?"

Grace smiled ruefully. "Once my head cleared, I came to realize that the women friends I had were all married to colleagues of my husband. I didn't have a single friend outside that circle."

"That life doesn't fit you anymore," Mary said, reflecting back at Grace.

"It's funny how it took his death to wake up to the truth about my life," Grace responded.

"Things change. If you wanna survive, you've gotta change with it."

"That sounds like the voice of experience."

"Life's not perfect," Mary shrugged.

"I'm sorry. Here I'm going on about my own troubles, and you've probably had it harder than me."

"There you go again. Life isn't easy for anyone."

"I know. It's just that it seems like some people are better at dealing with life's challenges than others. Someone's always been there to take care of things for me. I've never had to take care of myself before."

"Well, you're on your own now," Mary pointed out.

"It's not easy."

"Did you really think it would be?"

"That's the problem. I've never had to think about it at all."

Mary yawned. "You've got the rest of your life to figure it out."

"You're making me tired with that yawning," Grace said. "Maybe we should go to bed."

The new friends hugged, before they each went into their separate bedroom.

VIII

When Grace woke up the following morning, Mary had already left for the diner. She found a note on the kitchen table inviting her to stop in for breakfast whenever she was ready. Suddenly cheered that she that didn't have to eat another breakfast alone, she prepared to leave.

Grace found Mary run off her feet by the time she arrived at the diner. "Is everything OK?" Grace asked.

"Betty can't make it this morning. One of her kids is sick. It's just me and Janie, until Bob comes in for the lunch shift."

"Is there anything I can do?" Grace asked.

Hands on hips, Mary looked Grace up and down. "Do you know how to make coffee?"

"Probably not as well as you, but I'm sure I can manage."

"Good enough." Mary handed Grace an apron then turned away in response to the timer on the oven. She took out a batch of what smelled like steaming oatmeal muffins and placed them on the counter to cool. "Maybe after you're done making the coffee, you can give me a hand in the kitchen?"

"What do you want me to do?" Grace asked, once she'd mastered the coffee maker.

"You can whip up this pancake batter while I fire up the grill."

And so the morning went. The three women set about preparing breakfast for the clientele. When the customers started to arrive, Grace got a crash course in customer service. Janie handed her a note pad and pencil to write down her orders. Then she showed her where to clip them, on a line fixed up in the window, between the kitchen and dining area. She didn't do too badly at first. But when it started to get busy, she mixed up some of the orders and got backed up clearing away the dishes. And she certainly didn't have time to stack dishes in the dishwasher. Janie was able to pick up some of the slack, for which Grace was most grateful.

By the time Bob arrived at 10:30 a.m., there were only a few patrons left in the diner who lingered over their coffee. Mary came out of the kitchen, poured two cups of the dark blend, and handed one to Grace. "I could use a break."

"What about Janie?" Grace asked.

"She's gonna load the dishwasher first, then she'll come join us."

Grace took a sip of the life-sustaining tonic, before she noticed a man holding up his cup for more coffee. "I'd better get that."

When Mary saw who it was, she called out, "Can't you see we're on a break Tom? Why don't you just help yourself?"

"Oh sorry," Tom apologized. He got up to help himself and offered refills all around.

"Thanks Tom. That one's on the house," Mary said. She rubbed her forehead. "I knew I'd regret having that wine last night."

"You and me both," Grace said. "I think we're probably suffering from sleep deprivation as well. It was rather late by the time we got to bed."

"You think?"

Grace laughed. "Any regrets?"

Mary yawned. "Only about the wine."

"Don't start in with the yawning again. You know what happened last time."

"Oops, sorry. By the way, thanks for helping out this morning. You saved my bacon."

"You would have managed."

"You're kidding, right?"

"I sure am hungry," Grace said. "I never did get that breakfast you promised me. Want some toast?"

"With peanut butter?"

Grace got up to make it. "Coming right up."

"Hold on there. I'll make it. Like you said, I did promise to make you breakfast."

"Feel better?" Mary asked a little while later, when Grace washed down the last of her toast with coffee.

"Much," Grace said with a smile.

"Good, because I was hoping you wouldn't mind sticking around for the rest of the day."

The place was surprisingly busy for a little out-of-the-way diner. Many of the customers were local and seemed to use the diner as a place to catch up on gossip. But there was also a fair number of visitors to the area.

Grace was exhausted by the end of the day, but it was a good kind of tired. She agreed to help out again the Tuesday after the Victoria Day weekend.

As soon as she got home, she headed for the bathroom to fill a bowl with hot soapy water for her aching feet. It took a few minutes for her feet to adjust to the water temperature. But once she did, the tension in her body began to ease. She fell asleep. An hour went by before the chilled water woke her. Newly revived, she ate a simple dinner and spent the rest of the evening reading her book.

* * * * * *

Things went a little more smoothly her second day on the job. She was already becoming familiar with some of the names of the locals who ate there. They were a friendly bunch, and it was a pleasant atmosphere to work in.

Albert and Maggie turned up at lunch time.

"What can I get you?" Grace asked.

"I think I'll have the meatloaf," Maggie said absentmindedly. She closed the menu before she noticed her server was. "Grace. What are you doing here?"

"Mary's short-staffed right now and asked me to help out," she explained.

"How's that working out?" Albert wanted to know.

Grace turned to Albert. "It's only my second day, but I think it's going pretty well."

A bell rang signaling an order was ready. "I have to get that," Grace said after a quick glance. "What can I get for you Albert?" She took his order and clipped both to the line. She picked up the burger and fries and delivered it to George whose wife still hadn't returned from Sudbury.

"Would you like a refill on that coffee?" she asked.

"Please," he answered and held up his mug.

After she poured George's coffee, she rested her hand on the back of the booth opposite, and said, "You must get tired of eating in the diner all the time."

"It beats my own cooking." He took a bite of his burger and it dribbled down his mouth. He wiped it with a napkin.

"I was thinking maybe you could come to my place for dinner some time," she offered.

George choked on his burger.

"Are you all right?" Grace thumped him on the back.

He gulped his water, placed his large hands on either side of his plate, and regarded her. "I'm not sure that's entirely appropriate," he said.

"You're probably right," she answered looking around the diner. "Forget I said anything."

"Wait," he said.

Grace paused, turned, and walked slowly back to his table.

"I want to thank you for the offer. That was very kind," he said.

Somewhat mollified, Grace said, "I only meant to thank you for teaching me about the history of the area."

"I know." He looked around the room, leaned forward, and whispered, "Others may not understand."

Grace nodded. "You're right of course. If I were part of a couple..." she shrugged.

"Yes," he said. "Perhaps when my wife gets back," he suggested.

"Right. Well, I'd better get back to work."

While one dinner invitation fell through, another opportunity was provided by Albert and Maggie. "I'd love to come to dinner tonight," she said.

"Mary has already accepted our invitation, so perhaps you can come together," Maggie offered.

"Can I bring anything?" Grace asked.

"Mary has promised to save one of her apple pies."

"Well, I don't think I'll have time to prepare anything. How about if I bring the wine?"

"Sounds perfect. We'll look forward to seeing you both later," Maggie said and gave Grace a hug before leaving with Albert.

The diner closed at 4:00 pm, which gave Grace and Mary ample time to clean up, before they had to be at Maggie's.

"Is it like this every day?" Grace asked Mary when they locked up for the night.

"This is pretty much how it is in the summer time. In the winter, we just get the locals, so business slows down a bit. I do all right."

"Why don't you be at my place in half an hour, so we can walk over together?" Grace suggested.

"I'll be there," Mary answered.

* * * * * *

"Dinner will be ready shortly," Maggie said when she answered her door. "Do you want a drink before we eat?"

Mary and Grace looked at each other and started to laugh.

"Care to let us in on the little joke?" Albert asked from behind Maggie.

"It seems Mary can't hold her liquor very well," Grace teased.

"I'll just have a cola if you have it," Mary said.

"Since I brought the wine, I feel I should at least have one glass," Grace joked. "I've had a bit more experience handling my wine than Mary."

"Will you working at the diner permanently?" Maggie directed her question to Grace.

"Probably just until Betty comes back," Grace responded. "One of her kids has chicken pox, and she had to stay home for a few days."

Mary picked up the cola bottle and pressed it to her brow and neck. "She's doing a great job too."

"Being a mother of two sons, I've had a lot of experience waiting tables," Grace chuckled. "Besides, it feels good to be doing something useful."

"Do you really mean that?" Mary asked.

Grace paused in the middle of taking a sip of her drink. "Of course I do. Why do you ask?"

"Well, I could use another part-time waitress for the summer. What do you say?"

"I say you've just hired yourself a new waitress," Grace smiled and clinked her glass against Mary's bottle. "Here's to new beginnings."

"How's three days a week sound?"

"Wonderful. I love getting up in the morning and having something to look forward to. I'm amazed how many people come to eat there every day."

"There's nothing surprising about it. It's my coffee," Mary laughed.

"I've noticed George is there every day. Is that usual?" Grace asked.

"That will probably change when his wife gets back," Mary said.

"He must miss her an awful lot. He seems so lost."

Albert retrieved a bottle of beer from the refrigerator and opened it with a fizz. "Not all men are as advanced as me," he teased. "He's probably not used to fending for himself."

"I hope that's all it is. He's such a nice man, even though he seems a bit distracted at times."

"He's always been like that," Mary piped in.

"He reminds me of one of the professor's at Charles's school. I feel quite comfortable with him."

"George wouldn't hurt a flea," Maggie agreed.

"That's good to hear. Some men seemed to think that because I'm widowed, I'm lonely for male companionship. It's so nice to be with a man that I don't have to be on my guard with all the time."

"If any of the men at the diner get a fresh with you, just let me know, and I'll see to it that they're out on their rear," Mary exclaimed.

"I think I'd better learn to take care of it myself," Grace pointed out.

"What, and deprive me of the pleasure?" Mary teased.

"Has anyone along the river sent you a message from the boys?" Albert directed his question to Mary.

"Not in a few days. The last I heard, they were doing fine."

"You must miss them?"

"I do miss having the boys under foot, but it's been nice to have the occasional evening to make new friends." Mary smiled at Grace.

The sun was going down, so Grace and Mary couldn't stay much longer. As they walked back to Crow's Nest, Grace decided that she was rather enjoying this new rhythm she'd found at the French River. She loved the people, the landscape, and the peace she had found here.

Still in a reflective mood when she arrived back at the cabin, Grace picked up her journal to share her thoughts with Charles.

Dear Charles: May 21, 1963

There's a different rhythm, here at the French, that I find I rather like. It's as though I can be myself in ways that I couldn't in Toronto. I'm not sure exactly what it is. Maybe it's because the people are more in touch with nature here. It makes me want to slow down and enjoy it. I mean all I have to do is step outside, and it beckons me to be a part of it.

In the city, people are all about doing; here it seems to be more about being. Does that make any sense? I feel like I've been living in a fog, and I've only now started to wake up to a new rhythm. Well, not new exactly, but new to me.

There's still much I don't fully understand about where my life is heading right now, but perhaps it's best this way.

Grace placed the pen between her lips in silent contemplation, while she re-read her words. One of the things that she loved about writing was that it took her deeper inside herself. She was always able to find a new perspective on things whenever she wrote her thoughts down.

I feel like I'm traveling down an unfamiliar road, and I have no idea where it will lead me. But for the first time in my life, I'm OK not knowing. Yet, I sense I'm heading in the right direction. That sounds strange even to me. But there it is.

Good night my love,
Grace.

IX

When Grace received her first pay check, she grinned from ear to ear. "The last time I received one of these was maybe twenty years ago."

"You're kidding, right?"

"Sorry, but outside of the odd job while I was in university, that's it," she shrugged.

"You went to university?"

"Just for a couple of years. When Charles went for his PhD, we needed the extra money, so I quit."

"Telephone for you, Mary," Bob yelled from the kitchen.

"Oh no, I hope that isn't Betty calling to tell me she can't come back to work just yet," Mary said when she answered the phone.

When Grace picked up her order at the window, Mary was staring blindly at the phone hanging from her hand. "What's wrong?" she asked, her order forgotten.

Mary sat frozen in her seat.

Grace tried again. "Mary, you're scaring me. Tell me what's happened."

The touch of Grace's hand on Mary's seemed to bring her back to the present. She stared blankly at her friend. "It's David. He's been in a car accident."

"Is he all right?"

"He's dead." Once the words were said out loud, it opened up a dam of tears.

Grace hugged her friend and let her cry.

"Why don't you take her home," Bob said. "I'll take care of everything around here."

"That's a good idea. Come on Mary."

Grace guided Mary up the back stairs, to where she lived with her boys. Within a few minutes, she placed a heavily sweetened cup of tea into Mary's hands.

"I have to go and claim the body." Mary placed the tea on the kitchen table and rubbed her palms down her thighs, as though she was unsure what to do with her hands.

"Do you want me to go with you?"

"I don't know. Maybe someone ought to be here in case the boys come back. God, how am I going to tell them?" she sobbed.

"You don't have to decide anything right now," Grace said reassuringly.

Mary stared at the table for a long time. "I always thought that David would come back to us some day, you know?" The sobs rose and overflowed like water over the side of a glass.

Mary's tears cut Grace to the core. There were no words, so Grace just held her friend while she wept.

"I think I'd like to go and lie down for a while." Mary pushed herself up from the table and blundered down the darkened hallway.

Grace found Mary lying on top of the bed. She drew the curtains against the outside world and turned to tend to her friend. "Do you need a blanket?" she asked.

"Hallway cupboard," Mary sniffled.

Grace picked out a blanket from the linen cupboard and draped it over Mary. "Is there anything else you need?"

Eyes glistening, Mary grasped Grace's hand and hugged it to her chest. "Will you stay with me tonight?"

Grace sank down on the side of the bed. "Of course I will. I'll stay as long as you need me."

While Grace sat in the semi-darkness, she felt a light breeze on her face from the open window. A train whistle sounded in the distance. A dog barked. And there was an indistinct buzz of voices from below. As soon as her eyes adjusted to the light, she could make out the image of a photograph on the night table. She wanted to pick it up to get a closer look, but she didn't dare move in case it interrupted Mary's grief-stricken slumber. She leaned forward to get a better look. It appeared to be a sepia-toned wedding photo. She recognized a younger, slimmer, version of Mary in a simple off-white dress. It had puff sleeves, was fitted at the waist, and flowed gently past the knees. Her dark hair was pulled up at the sides, while the rest floated around her shoulders. She wore a sprig of wildflowers in her hair that complemented the bouquet in her hand. David stood beside her. He looked dark and mysterious, as he stared into the camera. Full lips hinted at a smile which heightened his cheek-bones. His suit was a heavy weave, probably wool, that looked to have seen a lot of wear. The collar of his white shirt crinkled at the neck, where it was pulled together with a collar pin. He wore a striped tie and a sprig of flowers in his lapel that matched Mary's bouquet.

Grace stared at the photograph for a long time then back at Mary's tear-stained face. She was asleep. Grace carefully released herself from Mary's slackened hand and slipped out of the room. She tried to keep her emotions in check while she cleaned up the dishes, but her tears had a life of their own. She knew only too well the pain her friend was going through.

Grace searched the bathroom cupboard for some aspirin. She swallowed two of the tiny pills with handfuls of cold water, then she squeezed out a wet terry cloth to dab her face and neck. The cool cloth felt good on her face and helped to ease the puffiness around her eyes. Unfortunately, it didn't ease the bone-deep tiredness she felt. She slept in the room across from Mary with the door ajar. She wanted to be available in case Mary needed her during the night. An hour later, still awake, she wandered into the kitchen in search of something to write on. Grace found a note pad and pen in the drawer under the kitchen table. She made herself comfortable on the living room couch and began to write by lamp light.

My Dearest Charles: May 24, 1963

My friend Mary just got a phone call that every woman dreads. Her husband David has died in a car accident. She's naturally heartbroken. I just wish there was something I could do to help. I suppose being here is something. But the truth is, there is no way but through the pain of suffering and loss. No-one escapes, though God knows I wanted to after I got the call. I suppose I succeeded to some extent by coming here to the French River. But even here the memories are strong.

It's funny how some of my most precious memories are of simple things — like conversations at the dinner table. Remember how the boys would talk over each other, but somehow we managed to understand every word? Then after dinner we would let them loose outside in the hope that they'd be worn out by bedtime. Even then, they'd fight sleep and stay awake long into the night. And how many times did their murmured voices spoil the mood? We'd lie there and talk, while we waited for them to drift off. Instead, we were the ones who were too tired to stay awake. We were so relieved they weren't fighting, we didn't have the heart to tell them to pipe down.

Oh Charles, it's so hard without you. Will there ever come a time when I can think of you without feeling like my heart is being ripped out? And do I ever want that time to come? Will it mean that I've forgotten you? At least the pain means you're still with me.

When I think about what Mary has ahead of her, my heart aches. And what of the boys? How are they going to feel when they find out their father has died? Although I haven't known them very long, I've come to care about these people. I know you'd care for them too if you could have only met them. I'm so glad to have you for my confidant.

All my love,
Grace.

When Grace walked into the kitchen the following morning, Mary was already there. "I didn't expect to see you up so soon," she said.

"I have to get an early start if I want to get to North Bay today."

"Are you sure you don't want me to go with you?"

"With Betty off, I need you to stay here to help Bob at the diner."

"Of course. What do you want me to do if the boys turn up while you're away?"

"I've called David's father, Henry. He's going to come and stay in case they return before I get back." She got up from the table and emptied the remainder of her coffee in the sink. "Well I'd better be going." She picked up the suitcase by the front door and walked out.

The diner felt empty without Mary's presence. Grace didn't even know where to start in her morning preparations. She couldn't seem to think straight. She managed to get the coffee on and the tables set before Janie and Bob appeared. She kept getting orders wrong, and once she even dropped the silverware. Everything had to be rewashed by hand which put her further behind. It didn't take long for word to get around about David's death. By noon, it seemed like the whole community was aware of it.

"Sit down for a few minutes," Janie said when she saw how flustered Grace was.

"I couldn't possibly," Grace answered.

"Of course you can." Janie pushed Grace through the door, situated at the back of the kitchen. "Take a few minutes to catch your breath."

As soon as her butt made contact with the bench shoved up against an outside wall, Grace's entire body drooped. She closed her eyes, leaned her head against the wall, and let the air cool her shattered nerves.

By the second day, Grace, Bob, and Janie were becoming accustomed to the reorganization of tasks without Mary. There were fewer mishaps, and the continued conversations about David's death didn't slam her like they did the previous day. If only the boys would come home.

When Mary arrived home two days later, she looked tired and gaunt. She'd made arrangements for the funeral to take place at Corpus Christi Parish on the Dokis Reserve.

Mary and David grew up on the island, were even married at the church there, so it held a special meaning for them.

In the days leading up to the funeral, things were busy at Mary's. People dropped by with food, and family members gathered to console one another.

Grace did her best to be a good friend to Mary, but she was glad to have the escape of work to help her deal with her own memories.

James and Will turned up the day before the funeral. Mary was naturally relieved that they'd returned in time to say goodbye to their father. Once the boys received news of their father's death, they rushed to their mother's side amidst tears and hugs.

The Corpus Christi Parish was a charming little white clapboard church that had served as a place of worship for the people of the Dokis Reserve since 1914. It was packed with friends and family members who had come to pay their respects.

After the service, everyone was invited for a buffet lunch in the church basement. Grace sat with Maggie and Albert along with a few other people she'd met since her arrival.

When Grace saw Mary standing at the buffet table with a half-filled plate of food in her hand, speaking to yet another mourner, she went over to help. "Excuse me, but there's someone over here who'd like to speak with you." Grace placed a supporting arm around Mary's waist and led her to their table.

"Thanks. I just need to sit down for a few minutes."

"Let me get you something to drink with that," Grace offered. "What would you like?"

Mary eased herself into a chair. "I could use a cup of coffee right about now."

By the time Grace returned, there was someone else occupying Mary's time. Grace maneuvered her way past the newcomers and placed the coffee in front of Mary.

Grace sat down to finish her own meal, while Mary continued to speak with one person after another. Their conversations seemed centered around memories of growing up on the island with David and Mary. She only half listened, as her gaze wandered. Will was in conversation with some friends on the other side of the room, while James stood alone a few feet away.

After lunch, many of the mourners began to disperse while family members, who hadn't seen each other in a long time, were invited back to the house. Grace decided it was a good time to leave.

"Why don't you come too?" Mary offered.

"Thank you. But I think you need this time to be with your family."

"You feel like family."

Grace placed a hand over her heart. "I don't know what to say."

"Say you'll come."

Despite Mary's assertion that she was like family, Grace felt out of place among these people. It wasn't that they were Native, it was just that she didn't have a history with these people. She sat and listened politely and laughed where appropriate, while everyone shared their memories of David. When she saw James slip out of the room, she decided to follow.

"Is everything all right?" Grace asked when she caught up with him in the kitchen, where he was searching the contents of the refrigerator.

He looked at her with mournful eyes. "Just thinking," he said.

"About your father?" Grace guessed.

He shut the refrigerator door and crossed his arms across this chest. "Maybe. Probably. I don't know."

Grace placed a hand on his arm to comfort him.

He flinched and took a step back. Clearly he didn't want to talk.

Grace pressed her lips together. "I'm here if you need someone to talk to."

Unable to look at her directly, he merely nodded.

"OK then," she said and went back into the living room to say her goodbyes. It really was time for her to go.

Grace heaved a sigh of relief when she shut the door of her camp. She plopped herself down in her favourite chair by the window and closed her eyes. Emotions bombarded her senses. She wanted to shield herself from it, but knew she couldn't. Bad things happened to good people. There was no rhyme or reason to it. Things happen, people adjust, and life goes on.

Outside the open window, a fog was moving in over the river, and with it a familiar serenade floated on a ribbon of air that enveloped Grace in its oddly comforting embrace.

X

Mary was already at the diner when Grace arrived the following morning. "What are you doing here?" Grace asked. "I would have thought you'd want to take some time off."

"I can't afford to take any more time off," Mary replied. She beat the pancake batter with a vengeance. "You know summer is our busiest season."

Grace took the beater out of Mary's hands. "But we have everything under control. You don't need to come back to work until you're ready."

"This place is my responsibility," she said and began to fill the jars of maple syrup for the tables.

"Look at you. Your hands are shaking so much you can't even fill those jars without spilling half of it." Grace gently removed the heavy bottle from Mary's hands. "Why don't you go home and get some rest."

"Look, David wasn't here before, so nothing's really changed, has it?" Mary clutched the counter with both hands, as though it might prevent her from falling.

"Technically no," Grace began...

"I don't have time to stand around here and argue," she shot back. "I have customers coming in soon, and there's still plenty to do."

Grace decided to let the matter drop for the moment. The time would come when she'd have no excuse not to rest.

Mary continued to push herself. There seemed little that Grace could do but wait and be there when Mary finally gave in. And she would. Of that, Grace was sure.

* * * * * *

That moment came early one morning, when someone pounded on Grace's front door.

"Who on earth," Grace mumbled sleepily. She wrapped herself in a robe and answered the insistent pounding.

"It's Mom. We can't get her out of bed," Will said, frantically.

Grace was instantly alert. "Has anyone called the doctor?"

"James has gone for him."

"I'll be there in a minute," Grace said and hurried into the bedroom to dress, while Will paced by the dock.

Grace tapped her foot on the bottom of the boat, while Will maneuvered through the swifts. This was always the part of the trip that slowed them down. But it was necessary to avoid hitting any of the rocks hidden beneath the water. When they finally arrived at their destination, they found James wearing out the living room carpet.

"How is she?" Grace asked.

"The doctor's with her now."

"Do you know what's wrong?"

"She's exhausted." Dr. Brody appeared around the corner. "She's just suffered a great loss, yet she won't give herself time to grieve. This is her body's way of shutting down, so that she can get the rest she needs."

"So, she will get better?" James wanted to know.

"She's a strong woman. With the proper rest and support, I have every reason to believe that she'll be fine."

"What about the state of her mind?" Grace asked, recalling her own difficulty accepting the loss of her husband.

"She needs to face her loss of course, but first she must rest. Then she can mourn."

"How can we help her?" Grace wanted to know.

"Let her sleep as much as she wants to. When she's ready, she'll start moving around again. Make sure she gets plenty of fluids — broth, water, juice — to keep up her strength and prevent her from getting dehydrated. I'll stop by in a couple of days to see how she's doing. If you need me before then, you know where to get a hold of me."

The boys looked relieved, when Grace offered to stay over.

Mary slept almost non-stop for two days, her bed became a haven of oblivion from her loss. She got up for short periods of time, to take care of only what was essential, and to sip the liquids Grace and the boys forced into her.

By the third day she was feeling a little better. Though still weak, she was able to sit up in bed and eat a little toast with her tea. But she tired easily and soon needed to lie down again.

After a week, Mary was doing much better physically, though she still wasn't ready to go back to work. Fortunately, Betty was back on the job, and Grace went in as often as she could when she wasn't helping to take care of Mary. By the second week, Mary was gaining strength and was able to get around and eat solid food. It was time for Grace to go home. Once there, she leaned against the door and wondered what to do with herself. Then she walked across the room, climbed fully clothed into her still unmade bed, pulled the covers over her head, and slept.

* * * * * *

When Grace opened the door to find James on her doorstep the following afternoon, she knew why he was there. During her stay to help take care of Mary, James had continued to be distant and pre-occupied with his thoughts. There were moments when she thought he was going to say something, but he stopped himself.

"Come on in." Grace stepped aside for him to enter. "How's your mother?"

"She's fine," he replied, absentmindedly. "Will is with her." He wandered around the room, as though he wasn't sure what to do with himself.

"Can I get you anything?"

"Huh?"

"Follow me." Grace headed for the kitchen. "Sit down while I get us both a cola."

He accepted the proffered bottle and took a perfunctory sip. He leaned forward in the chair with the bottle cradled in his hands. "You know she tries to be strong for Will and me, but I know it's not easy for her."

"No, I don't suppose it is. But at the same time, you and Will give her a reason to go on."

James nodded, while he wrung the bottle with his hands.

"How are you doing?" Grace asked.

He seemed surprised by the question. He sat up straight, placed the coke on the table, and wiped his wet hands on his denim-clad thighs. "Me? I'm fine."

"Well, you're doing better than I am, then," Grace said quietly.

He looked puzzled. "What do you mean?"

"Well, you've just lost your father a few weeks ago, and you're fine. I lost my husband a few months ago, and I'm still not fine."

"How long does it take?"

"In some ways, you never really get over the loss, but I understand that it becomes easier to live with over time."

"Is that true?"

"I'll let you know."

He shot out of the chair and began to pace, stopped, started again, and then ran his fingers through his hair. "I don't know how I'm supposed to feel right now. My father's

dead. I know I should mourn him, but for some reason..."
He shrugged.

Grace waited patiently for him to continue.

"I remember him, and I don't. Do you know what I mean? I remember him being home, but I only have a vague memory of what he was like. It's as though everyone around me is talking about a stranger."

"What is your vague memory of your father?"

"What?" James paused in mid stride and turned to face Grace.

"You said you had a vague memory of your father. What is it?"

James frowned, and his eyes narrowed, while he searched his memories. He walked over to the window and leaned against the frame. As he looked out, a slight smile touched his face. His eyes softened. "I do remember my father taking me out into the woods to teach me about nature." He turned to her with his next words. His eyes glowed with the memory. "He had this amazing connection to it. It's like he wanted to share that with me. I guess he's the reason I love the outdoors so much," James continued. "But what I remember most about that time was being happy when I was with him."

"Sounds like he shared the best part of himself with you," Grace said quietly.

James raised his eyebrows, as though he was surprised with the truth of her words. "You're right," he acknowledged. "I never thought of that before."

* * * * * *

After James left, Grace decided to take a walk to clear her thoughts. Despite all that had happened, she was glad she decided to come to the French River. She felt more involved in life here. She knew she would have to go back to Toronto some time. But for now, she could pretend that her real life was here.

The resinous aroma of indigenous pine trees hung in the humid air and clung to her body. It amazed her how the trees seemed to lean in the same direction in this part of the country. It was as though they were held in some kind of traction, but she knew it was the wind that bent them just so. The sight brought to mind one of her favourite paintings by Frederick H. Varley called *Stormy Weather* which was painted further along the river at Georgian Bay.

When a buzzing sound caught her attention, her eyes scanned the landscape to discover the fluttering wings of a Ruby-throated Hummingbird hovering over a Cardinal flower. She watched it for a while then moved on.

When she stepped out of the sunshine into the woods, she shivered at the difference in temperature. Once her eyes adjusted to the change of light, she could make out ferns growing wild, amidst fallen pine needles, at the base of the trees. And the fecund fragrance of earth filled her nostrils, when her feet stirred up the ground.

When Grace found herself at the Williams camp, she realized that's where she was headed all along. When no one answered her knock on the screen door, she leaned over to peek inside. But all she saw were silent dust motes, floating on streams of sunlight, through the north-west window. Just as she was about to head home, she heard someone call out to her from among the trees.

"Are you looking for me by any chance?"

Grace recognized Maggie's voice immediately, but it took a moment to locate her. "I might have known you'd be out in the woods painting," Grace teased when Maggie came into view.

"Not today I'm afraid. I'm picking berries. This is the extent of my culinary skills." She held up a pail of bright red raspberries and offered one to Grace.

Grace popped one of the sun-warmed morsels into her mouth and felt its furry texture brush against her tongue. "Mmmm, this is delicious. What are you planning to do with them?"

"I'll probably just serve them on ice cream for dessert tonight," Maggie said as they wandered into the cozy kitchen, where she placed the pail of berries on the counter. "How's Mary doing?"

Feeling right at home, Grace filled the kettle with water and set it on the stove. "She seems to be doing better. In some ways she's lost David twice. Once when he walked out on the family, and again when she heard that he wouldn't ever be coming back."

"True, true. But Mary's a strong woman. She'll come through all right."

"Yes, I believe you're right about that."

"Losing a husband is a terrible thing at such a young age. It's going to take some time to get over it. But I don't have to tell you that, do I?"

"Why do you suppose I'm worried?" Grace helped herself to the cookies from the cookie jar and handed one to Maggie. "I remember all too well how it feels."

"You'll both find your way and be the stronger for it," Maggie said. When the kettle whistled, Maggie took a quick bite of her peanut butter cookie and completed the preparations for tea.

"I know. But Maggie's not the only one I'm worried about. James came to see me earlier."

Maggie joined Grace at the kitchen table. "Oh?"

"He's doing his best to keep it together for his mother, but he's struggling with his feelings about his father."

"It's been hard on those boys. They've had to grow up awfully fast," Maggie pointed out. "Mary's done a fine job with them though. She's been both a father and a mother to them."

"I guess it's better than having a man around who wasn't able to be the father they needed."

Maggie dunked her cookie into her tea to soften it. "David Whitefeather will always be remembered as a good man, despite the fact that he had difficulty adjusting to life after the war."

Grace watched Maggie scoop the dissolving cookie into her mouth. "What was he like?"

"He was very responsible and caring like James. He loved the land. It's so sad what war does to good men."

"I saw a picture of him on Mary's nightstand. He certainly was a serious looking fellow," Grace said.

"He was that. But handsome too, I'd say — in a dark brooding kind of way."

"You make him sound like Heathcliff from *Wuthering Heights*."

Maggie chuckled. "A lot kinder if you ask me."

Albert entered through the screen door with a lot of clatter. He carried a fishing rod in one hand and a string of catfish in the other. He gave the two women a greeting on his way to the kitchen, where he placed the fish for cleaning. He washed his hands, with a squeezed lemon to get rid of the fishy smell, and sauntered over to the table. "Staying for dinner?" he smiled at Grace. "We've got plenty."

"I was hoping you'd ask," Grace smiled.

As always, Grace's had a lovely evening with Maggie and Albert. She wasn't the least bit tired when she got home later that evening, so she sat reading for a while. But her thoughts started to stray to Albert and Maggie's unique relationship. The best way to sort out her thoughts was to get them down on paper.

Dear Charles: June 20, 1963

I just got back from visiting Albert and Maggie. I told you about them. They're such an interesting couple. I wish I'd met them years ago. They have the kind of relationship I never dreamed two people could have. Would you believe that Maggie doesn't cook? It's true. Albert takes care of it for her and seems happy enough to do so. I never would have dreamed of asking you to cook dinner. Although it would have been nice to have your help from time to time. Thinking back, I don't know why I never complained about it. But I guess it's because you worked, and I stayed home. I felt it was my responsibility to take care of everything else. I never told you how much I resented being stuck in the kitchen, while everyone else visited during family gatherings. It would have been so nice if you could have helped out during those times. But I was brought up to believe that it was my job to take care of such things. Well, apparently it doesn't have to be that way. Things are changing, and I plan to be on board. Maggie is my inspiration.

Do you remember when women filled in for the men during the war? They learned how to build bombs, fly planes, work in stores, and generally help out wherever there was a need. And what's more, women liked it. But did anyone consider their feelings when the men came back from the war? No. Women were herded right back into the kitchen whether they wanted it or not. Did anyone even say thanks? Did anyone consider they might have enjoyed the independence and want to keep it? Instead, they not only had to adjust to being servile again, they had to tend to those men who were broken by the war like David was. Where's the justice in any of that? Who tended the wounds of disappointment brought about by being forced back into the home?

Sometimes, I wish I had taken on a man's work, like so many other women, instead of knitting socks and writing letters to the men overseas. If only I could have made you understand why I wanted more for myself. Maybe I'd be better able to cope now. But I didn't fully understand myself. Not then. It wasn't until after the war that I began to appreciate the importance of having my own income. I wanted to be able to contribute something. I know it wouldn't have been much, but it would have been mine. I wanted to make friends that weren't affiliated with the university. I wanted to be more than just a wife and mother. Can you understand that Charles?

I suppose none of that matters now. It's just that now that I know how it can be, there's no turning back.

Grace.

XI

Grace knocked on Mary's door and waited. Just when she thought no one would answer, the door burst open, and there stood Mary. "Is everything all right?" Grace asked.

"Sorry, I was in the middle of something." Mary stood to one side of the door and allowed Grace to enter. "Sit down."

"Is this where your mind has been?" Grace asked when she saw the photo albums strewn about the kitchen table. "May I?" She motioned to the album closest to her.

"Help yourself." Mary handed Grace a cup of coffee and sat down opposite.

Grace began to turn the pages of the album in front of her. When she came to a photo of David, she said, "You can see where the boys get their good looks." She turned the album and pointed to the picture in question.

Mary leaned across the table to get a better look. "Ah yes, that was taken at a family gathering. One of David's uncles came to visit that summer, so there was a big cook out. David prepared a spit for the pig."

"You cooked an entire pig?"

"It was the easiest way to feed everyone. All the families were there." Tears welled in Mary's eyes at the memory of happier times.

Grace placed a comforting hand over her friend's, and said, "Will you tell me about him?"

"Well," Mary began. "I've known David since we were both kids. We grew up together on the reserve. David was always getting me out of scraps."

"You were a handful even then?" Grace teased.

"I was small for my age, so I had to make up for it by being tough. We hung around with the same crowd, you see. We'd swim and fish together," she chuckled. "The boys even taught us girls how to put a worm on a hook. Of course, David was the one to show me how it was done. I didn't want to it. It gave me the shivers."

"You? I thought you were so tough?" Grace laughed.

"Only on the outside," she qualified. "Anyway, I didn't want to disappoint him, so I did it."

Clearly Mary was proud of her accomplishment, so Grace smiled her encouragement.

"Then one night, after we got done eating our catch, I went into the woods to relieve myself, and David followed." Mary's voice rose. "I was so mad at him. I accused him of spying on me and swatted him one." She demonstrated her technique with a swing of her arm. "He fell backwards." Mary snickered. "I guess he wasn't expecting to be attacked by a crazy woman." She blushed. "Turned out he was just trying to keep me safe. I told him I didn't need taking care of anymore." Mary leaned forward and whispered. "Secretly I was thrilled, but I didn't tell him that."

"How old were you?" Grace asked.

"Mmmm," Mary calculated. "Maybe fifteen."

Grace's hand rested on the photo. "He sounds like a very special person."

"Here, let me get you some more coffee," Mary said. She added two teaspoons of sugar and a dollop of milk to her cup and stirred up memories along with her coffee. "Later that night we all went swimming, like we always did after a cook out. The stars were so bright. I remember floating out there on my back enjoying the view. Then, that nasty boy grabbed me around the waist and pulled me under. I swallowed a bunch of water and started pounding him. I called him all manner of names."

Grace chuckled. "Even then, you liked to speak your mind."

"Damn right." Mary nodded. "I couldn't let him get away with that." Her voice softened. "But you know happened next?"

Grace could only guess. "He kissed you," she said softly so as not to break the spell.

"That came later. No, he grabbed me around the waist and tried to stop my arms from flapping about. But the feel of his wet body, smashed up against mine, made me think about things that would shock my mother. I couldn't help it. In that moment everything changed between us." Her voice trailed off. Mary was no longer in the present. She was in another time, when life was carefree and happy.

Grace allowed her eyes to be drawn to the sunshine, where it cast its rays through the strawberry covered curtains, onto the vanilla walls. A silver toaster kept company with a flowered canister set on the limited counter space, and a cozy-covered teapot sat by the stove ready for the next pot to be brewed.

"I've got to get out of here," Mary said out of nowhere.

"Huh? What?" Grace was startled out of her reverie.

"We're going for a walk," Mary reiterated on her way out the door.

Grace rushed down the stairs, into the sunlight, and caught a glimpse of Mary before she disappeared down the winding tree-covered path that lead to the marina. By the time Grace caught up with her at the dock, Mary had already shucked her sandals and was dangling her feet in the water. Still panting from her exertion, Grace was slow to join her friend.

Mary stared fixedly at the channel that eventually opened into the river and went all the way to Alberta. "David loved it here."

"James told me he was a guide," Grace said.

"A good one too. He could take people out in all kinds of weather — winter through summer. Whether they wanted to go hunting, fishing, or just learn about the area, David was the one to do it. We didn't have much, but we were happy." She swirled her feet in the clear water. "Damn that war anyway."

"I can't argue with that," Grace said softly. She watched an otter swim across the channel, its dark face and small eyes visible above the water, before it dove out of sight on the other side. Two turkey buzzards floated across the sky swaying back and forth across each other's path.

Mary's feet beat fiercely against the water getting them both wet. "Damn, damn, and double damn."

A startled Grace asked, "What's the matter?"

"If it wasn't for that damn war, my life with David might still be here."

"So many good men lost," was all Grace could think to say.

"You got that right," Mary said angrily. "That bloody war took two people I loved."

Grace sat back in surprise. "Two?"

"David's brother died in that war as well." Mary glared off into the distance. "Bill was younger than David, but do you think that stopped him?" Mary shook her head in frustration. "He was too young and far too bloody reckless." She wiped her eyes on the back of her hand and sniffled.

Grace touched Mary's arm lightly. "You don't have say any more if you don't want to."

"David didn't even know that Bill had joined up until their paths crossed in France," Mary continued, as though she couldn't stop the words from pouring out. "They were in a foxhole one night. Bill got careless and lit a cigarette.

David tried to shove him out of the way, but a German bullet got him."

"Oh my God!" Grace whispered. "I'm so sorry." As thunder rumbled in the distance, Mary let loose huge guttural sobs that would, in time, help to wash away her grief. All Grace could do was hold on, until the storm subsided.

"I'm sorry," Mary snuffled. She sat back and wiped her red-rimmed eyes with the edge of her T-shirt.

"There's no need to be," Grace said. "Although I do wish I had brought a handkerchief." She lifted her wet blouse away from her body to show the evidence of Mary's outpouring.

Mary snickered through her tears, and Grace was only too happy to have been the cause of it.

"When David finally came home at the end of the war, he was a stranger." Mary continued her story. "He'd been fighting too long and seen too much. He tried to pick up where he left off," she shrugged. "Then the nightmares started. He scared the shit outta me one night, when he woke up and yelled, 'Get down you fool.' He practically shoved me off the bed, and there I was pregnant with James at the time. He felt so guilty, he started sleeping in the next room."

Another boat wended its way toward the dock. Two men unloaded their fishing tackle along with a hamper of food. Their voices carried across the water, as they kibitzed about who'd made the biggest catch.

One of them called out, as he held up his catch, with a huge grin on his face. "Great day for fishing," he said.

"Do you know them?" Grace asked.

Mary shook her head. "Never seen them before."

"Do you mind my asking?" Grace said after a while. "What made David leave?"

"Booze."

Grace was taken aback. "Oh dear."

"He said it made him feel better."

"But it didn't," Grace guessed.

"I think it did at first. Then he needed more and more. I tried to get him to stop, but between the nightmares and the guilt, he just couldn't seem to. Or maybe he didn't want to." She paused. "One night he came home and started yelling and carrying on. I was afraid he was going to hurt me." Mary swallowed. "Just give me a minute." Mary ran her hands over her knees and rocked back and forth. She watched Grace's reaction, as though she was begging her not to judge David too harshly. "It was so unlike him. He left the next morning."

"There was no other way?"

"We did try again." She shrugged. "We managed to have a few more years together. But it was just too hard. He knew he had to leave," Mary said softly.

Before Grace could respond, the rain started to come down in large spaced out drops. The wind stirred their hair. They scrambled to put their wet feet into their sandals and made a mad dash to the marina for shelter. A bolt of lightning shot across the sky and illuminated the dim interior. They stood in the doorway and watched the rain come down hard and heavy, then quickly pass, like the torrent of tears recently shed by Mary. It seemed like a good omen when the clouds moved on and left behind only blue skies.

"Let's go," Mary said, as soon as the rain stopped.

They retraced their steps along the tree-lined path. Huge drops of water plopped down on their heads from the over-hanging foliage, while mud oozed between the toes of their sandal-clad feet. They were drenched by the time they made it back to Mary's place. They stopped at an outside faucet, to rinse their muddy feet, before entering the back door to Mary's apartment. Once inside, Mary dashed into the bathroom to grab a towel for Grace. "I'll be out in a minute," she said and shut the door.

Grace dried off as best she could.

"Your turn," Mary said when she came out of the bathroom and handed Grace a terry robe.

A few minutes later, Grace joined Mary in the kitchen, where she was pouring two glasses of lemonade. "Feel better?" Mary asked.

"Much." Grace accepted the lemonade which she pressed to her cheek and forehead before taking a swallow. There was a quality to Mary that Grace couldn't quite put a name to — an anxious foreboding of something more to come. "What is it?" she asked.

"What makes you think something's wrong?" Mary stammered.

"I don't know. There just is."

Mary wrapped her arms around her torso, unable to look Grace in the eye. Then she spoke in a subdued voice, "You know when I told you that David died in a car accident?"

"I remember," Grace said quietly.

"Well, there's more." Mary turned to face Grace. "What I didn't tell you — what I didn't tell anyone, was David's accident involved him and a tree."

"What are you saying?"

"I don't know. I just keep thinking about what David said the day he left." Mary got up from her chair and walked over to the kitchen sink, grabbed a hold with both hands, and pressed herself up against the white porcelain. She turned abruptly and leaned back into it for support. She peered at Grace from across the room and spoke quietly. "He said that he didn't deserve to live."

"I don't understand?"

"I think that David wanted to do away with himself." The kitchen clock ticked off the seconds, as Mary awaited Grace's response.

"What did the police say?" Grace said guardedly.

"That it was drunk driving."

"Is there any reason not to believe that?"

Mary pushed herself away from the sink and sat back down across from Grace. "Well, he drank because he blamed himself for his brother's death."

"That doesn't necessarily mean he would kill himself."

"How can I know for sure?" she cried.

Grace put her arms around the other woman's shoulders and felt her sobs. "When people are upset, they say things they don't mean."

"But what if he really did mean it?" Mary pleaded.

Grace took Mary firmly by the shoulders and made eye contact. "You'll never know for sure, so why torture yourself when you can make a choice to believe otherwise?"

Mary pushed herself away from Grace. "Maybe you're right."

"I know I'm right. And what's more, you know it too. Don't be like David and blame yourself for something you had no control over."

* * * * * *

Later that night, Grace stared down at the lined pages of her journal. How was she supposed to make any sense of the complex emotions of this particular day? After some thought, she picked up her pen and began to write:

Dear Charles: June 21, 1963

How does one accept the unacceptable? How does one get over the death of a loved one? Perhaps you never do. Maybe the best you can hope for is for the pain to lessen over time. But what if the loss is beyond all comprehension? What if, like Mary's husband David, your nights are bombarded with mental images that haunt you?

I cannot imagine what it would be like to fight in a war -- to see friends die on the battlefield. Worse yet, to have a beloved brother die in your arms and feel that you are the cause. All your life you have tried to protect him. But how do you protect someone from an enemy bullet?

That is exactly what happened to Mary's husband. He did his duty as a soldier, but the price he paid was too high. In war, the price is always too high. Lots of women lost a loved one in the war. Those that never came back — and the ones that did, are often no less lost to their families.

And now Mary is left to deal with the intolerable. She must come to terms with the notion that David took his own life rather than live with the alternative. There are no answers, only questions. And so, I too, must accept that there is no order to everything in this life. All that is left is acceptance.

Grace.

XII

"Can you stick around after work?" Mary asked Grace a week after her revelation about David. "There's something I wanna ask you."

Grace's curiosity was piqued. "Sure," she replied.

"Harry Stonecalfe came to see me last night," Mary said without preamble, as soon as the front doors were locked for the night.

Grace placed her purse on the counter and walked over to her friend. "Who's Harry Stonecalfe?"

"He's a medicine man. He wants to know if I'd like to do a sweat."

"I've heard of those. How do you think it will help?"

"After our conversation the other day, I realized that I need to let go of my thoughts surrounding the circumstances of David's death. Mr. Stonecalfe thinks that a sweat will help me to sort things out. But I don't want to do it on my own."

Grace nodded. "Sounds reasonable."

Mary took a step toward Grace. "I'm glad you think so, because I want you to do it with me."

Grace was surprised by this revelation. "What? Why?"

"I figure both of us could use help letting go of some stuff from the past."

Intrigued, but uncertain, Grace wandered across the linoleum floor deep in thought. She paused and looked back at Mary. "But would he even let me participate?"

"I've already thought of that. Mr. Stonecalfe has agreed to allow you to be a part of the ceremony."

"Are you sure you want me? Wouldn't it be better to ask someone who is Ojibwe?"

"I don't want anyone else. I want you," Mary said emphatically. When Grace didn't immediately say no, Mary added, "At least talk to Mr. Stonecalfe before you decide."

"I'll talk to him," Grace relented. "But let's be clear. I'm not promising anything."

"Good," Mary answered. "Because we're meeting him in half an hour."

As soon as they walked up the path to Harry Stonecalfe's front door, he stepped out onto the porch with a big smile on his face. He was a large man who looked to be about forty. He wore a blue bandana around his short brown hair, and the lenses of his oversized glasses covered his full cheeks. But it was his eyes that caught Grace's attention. The brown was so dark that the pupils were almost invisible. It was quite disconcerting — almost as if he could see into her soul.

"Welcome." He enveloped each of them in his brawny arms. Grace felt his big round belly press into her middle.

With a sweep of his massive hand, he indicated the wicker furniture on the porch for their comfort.

"Well, Mr. Stonecalfe," Grace began, once they sat down. "Mary has been telling me about this sweat lodge ceremony she wants me to be a part of. Before I decide, I'd like to find out more about it."

Mr. Stonecalfe nodded.

"It seems like such a sacred ritual."

"This is true."

Grace waited, hoping he would expand on his all too brief comment. When nothing more was forthcoming, she asked, "I just wondered why I'm being allowed to participate?"

"Because you are seeking guidance," he said.

There it was again — that all-knowing look into her soul. Did he know something she didn't? Her eyes darted around the property taking in the rocks, the trees, and their boat down by the jetty. She toyed with the crucifix around her neck. "But I'm Catholic."

"So am I," Mr. Stonecalfe replied.

"You know I am," Mary piped in. "It's my faith that keeps me grounded during the rough stretches."

Grace looked from one person to the other. "I'm confused. If you're both Catholic, how can you...?"

"How can we participate in a Native ritual?" Mr. Stonecalfe finished. "One does not cancel out the other. There are many commonalities," he smiled. "For example, the birth of Christ corresponds with the eastern doorway, or sunrise — a new beginning. The death of Christ is likened to the western doorway, or sunset — a tribute to the past and to the spirits. Both will play an integral part in the ceremony. The medicine wheel speaks of acceptance of other people's faith. Unless you don't think you can accept our Native faith?"

"That sounds like a challenge, Mr. Stonecalfe," Grace said with a wry smile.

"As you wish," he smiled back.

"It never occurred to me that our faiths would have any similarities. It's an intriguing notion. Perhaps you'd better tell me more about this ceremony," Grace acquiesced.

"What would you like to know?"

"I'm particularly interested in what happens once you enter the sweat lodge."

"Of course." He nodded with his whole body. "Doing a sweat helps to bridge the gap between the natural world and the spirit world," he explained. "Those who participate are usually seeking some kind of healing or guidance. Once you are settled, the spirits will be called forth by means of prayers, chanting, and drumming. Each part of the ceremony has significance. The drum, for instance, is made from all of Creation and is the heart beat of Mother Earth.

"Throughout the ceremony, cedar water will be sprinkled on the hot rocks — one for each of the directions. This creates a cleansing steam. Each person will have a chance to speak or pray, if they want to. At the end of the ceremony, the spirits are thanked and sent home."

Grace contemplated his words before speaking. "What should I pray about?"

"You will know when the time comes. Afterwards you may wish to share your experience with myself, or a friend, to help you understand the message given to you by the Great Spirit."

"What do you mean, a message from the Great Spirit?" Grace asked.

"As I said earlier, people who enter the sweat lodge are seeking guidance. Whatever needs attending to will come up during the ceremony. All you have to do is to wait, and listen for guidance."

"Suppose I don't receive a message?"

Mr. Stonecalfe shrugged slightly. "Either way, you will feel the healing energies of Creation. All will be well."

"Just like that?" Grace said.

"It is so. As a Catholic, you have faith that God will show you the answer to your prayers, do you not?"

"Well, yes," Grace lied.

"Faith is all that is needed."

Grace wasn't so sure.

"God is available to all who seek his guidance, whether it is through a priest or through a medicine man." Mr. Stonecalfe smiled. "You will maintain your free will. If you need to leave the lodge, no one will think less of you. We only ask that you wait until the flaps are open in between rounds."

"Rounds?"

"There are four intervals of 20-30 minutes. Each interval is called a round."

"That's a long time to be sweating isn't it?"

"After the end of each round, the flaps will be opened to allow for the air to circulate. At this time, you may wish to drink some water to replace lost fluids."

"I see. Interesting," Grace murmured.

"So, will you join me?" Mary asked.

Two pair of eyes awaited Grace's response. The problem was she lacked the faith. She hardly ever went to church any more. Since Charles died, her faith had been sorely tested. *But this isn't church*, a voice whispered in her head.

"Have faith in the Great Spirit," Mr. Stonecalfe said.

Then, without knowing what she was saying, the words tumbled out of her mouth. "All right," Grace agreed.

While in bed that night, Grace tried, in vain, to read. She had no idea why she agreed to be part of a sweat, when she wasn't even sure she believed in God any more. She closed her book and place it on the nightstand.

Dear Charles: June 28, 1963

You'll never believe what I did today. In an effort to expand my horizons, I've agreed to take part in an Ojibwe sweat ceremony. Mary says it will help me to let go of some things from my past. The trouble is, it will entail having a bit of faith. That's something I'm in short supply of nowadays. Ever since you passed away, I haven't wanted to go to church, which is sad because my faith was always such a comfort to me. But no amount of prayers or faith can ever bring you back.

I've always believed that there's a reason for everything in life, but what could possibly be the reason for God to take you away from me before your time? I know we all have to die sooner or later, but later is always the best in my opinion. After, it is hoped, a full life has been lived. That's the key isn't it -- to live a full life — so that when your time comes, there are no regrets?

Perhaps that's why I agreed to do this sweat. I don't want to look back with the regret of a missed opportunity. Besides, without knowing how, I perceive that this is the path to my future. Does that make any sense? I know, it doesn't make much sense to me either, but maybe that's where faith comes in.

It occurs to me, that I am one of the Stick-Wavers that George told me about — one of the Catholic missionaries who came to the French River to convert the Natives to Christianity. Except now, I am the one being asked to explore the Native perspective on religion. How strange that a piece of the French River history should come full circle in this way four-hundred years later.

Goodnight sweetie,

Grace.

XIII

The day before the sweat, Grace and Mary were asked to fast for twenty-four hours and to sit in silent contemplation of the sacred event. Only then would they be ready to gather in front of the dome-shaped sweat lodge. The structure was made of jack pine saplings covered with blankets to keep out the sun and hold in the steam. Grace and Mary watched as Mr. Stonecalfe purified the tobacco with smudging and prayers to the Great Spirit. They learned that the pipe represented prayers in physical form. The smoke symbolized the words that reached out and touched everything. It connected the physical and spiritual world and set the intent. The fire in the pipe was the same fire that was in the sun — the source of all life. When the pipe was passed around in a clockwise direction, each women took a puff and said a silent prayer. Upon receiving the pipe, Mr. Stonecalfe dismantled it and returned it to its pouch, where it would sit until it was ready to be used again.

A continuation of the cleansing ritual followed, as Mr. Stonecalfe wafted the smoke of burning sweet grass over Mary and Grace with an eagle feather. They were ready to enter the lodge from the East — the beginning of new life — in a clockwise direction. Once inside, they bowed to the Great Spirit which brought them into close contact with Mother Earth. They sat cross-legged on the ground, their backs to the lodge poles, in comfortable shorts and T-shirt. It was now time for the fire keeper to bring in the hot stones. The spirit of the stones, called Grandfathers, had been awakened in the fire then swept clean with a cedar bough to remove smoking embers that might cause irritation. One at a time, the seven Grandfathers, one for each direction: North, South, East, West, Up, Down, and Center, were placed in the shallow pit inside the lodge. The first round of the sweat, honouring Mother Earth, which included: fire, rocks, water, and steam, was about to begin.

Gifts of tobacco, presented to the sweat leader, epitomized a person's spirit. Its roots went deep into the earth, and its smoke rose high into the heavens. It opened the door to the spirit world and allowed communication to take place on behalf of the person who needs healing.

Once settled inside the lodge, the entrance flap was closed leaving them in total darkness. The womb of Grandmother Earth, as the lodge is known by the Anishinaabe, was so thick with heat it was difficult to breathe.

They'd been asked to remove their jewelry while in the sweat lodge, as it could burn the skin. This also meant removing their wedding rings, which left Grace feeling like she was lacking in some way — no longer part of a whole.

It made Grace want to reach over and grab Mary's hand, so she felt less alone, but touching wasn't allowed.

Grace trembled, as she struggled to take in quick short bursts of the moist air. She tried to relax, but her heart pounded against her chest, and the dark unfamiliar surroundings made it difficult for her to obey the dictates of her mind. What she really wanted was to escape, to tell Mr. Stonecalfe that she had changed her mind. She thought she could do this, now she wasn't so sure.

Mr. Stonecalfe sprinkled cedar water onto the stones. There was a hiss followed by an unbearable rush of hot vapour that filled and surrounded her. When Grace's eyes began to adjust to the dark, she was finally able to see the other two occupants in the dull glow cast by the hot rocks.

As a signal for the spirits to enter the lodge, Mr. Stonecalfe's began the ceremony by letting out a deep rumble from his chest and allowing it to spill from his throat. Was that her own heart beating, or was it the heartbeat of Mother Earth vibrating through her body? Grace looked around the lodge unsure of what to expect. Would she be able to sense spirits in this place? She didn't know if she wanted to. She had visions of frightening apparitions slipping into the lodge intent on hurting her. In order to offset her fear, she tried to find comfort in the sound of Mr. Stonecalfe's gravelly voice. It seemed to help for a while. Then Grace's thoughts began to wander aimlessly. She felt at odds with her relief that nothing was happening, while at the same time she was left wanting.

Images of her life after her husband's death floated in and out of Grace's mind. She thought about the loneliness and fear now that her life had changed so irrevocably. And what about the sleepless nights that she lay awake and worried about how she was going to manage on her own? She had been totally unprepared to live a life without her husband.

Just as she was becoming accustomed to the unfamiliar surroundings, the flap was lifted to allow the air to circulate. She couldn't believe that the first twenty-minute round was over. The two women took the opportunity to refresh themselves outside and drink some water. Meanwhile, the fire keeper replaced the Grandfathers with new stones from the fire as would happen after each round. Grace knew that she could leave if she wanted to, but some force beyond her understanding made her re-enter the lodge.

During the second round, honouring the sisters, Grace was able to slip more easily into the rhythm of the chant. Her own puny sound got lost within Mr. Stonecalfe's deeply roughened voice. But she soon gained confidence, and her voice strengthened. She felt lifted and carried with the reverberation of their combined voices, along with the pulse of the Mother. Sweat dripped down her face, and pooled between her breasts, as cedar water sizzled on the rocks.

For the third round, honouring the brothers, Grace stumbled back into the lodge under a power that was not her own. When Mr. Stonecalfe invited more spirits into the lodge, her own voice began to weaken. Deeper and wider she slipped. She was no longer aware of her corporeal form, or the fact that her white cotton T-shirt clung to her body. She sang from somewhere deep inside her chest, while she swayed in time to the beat of the drum.

It was during the fourth and final round, honouring the self, that Grace surrendered. She was beyond individual thought, as she slipped into ubiquity.

Her body felt lighter and more fluid. It was like she was being lifted out of herself to another place — another way of being. She looked back to see herself seated before the shallow pit of hot stones. The sight should have shocked her, but she felt only calm. How strange.

Somehow, her spirit body passed through the lodge and floated higher across what seemed like time and space. Then a vision of her husband appeared. Overjoyed to see him again, she reached out to touch him. She may have even called his name out loud, she wasn't sure. They were in the middle of a field with his body pressed against hers. When they hugged, it felt real. His arms were so familiar to her. If this was heaven, she didn't think she ever wanted to leave. She asked the question that was foremost in her mind. "Why did you have to die?"

He looked down at her and smiled. "No one ever truly dies," he said.

"How can you say that?"

"But it's true. I'm right here. I'll always be right here."

"You're not listening to me. You're dead?" She punched him. His body felt solid. "I need you with me."

"You're the one who hasn't been listening," Charles pointed out with infuriating calm.

"I heard you. I just don't believe."

"Perhaps that's where the problem lies."

"What are you talking about?"

"You can create a new life for yourself," he said.

"How can I?"

"You can do whatever you want."

"Except be with you."

"We'll always be together."

"So you keep saying." She started to cry.

Charles's image began to fade, as she felt herself being pulled away from him. "Don't go!" she called out to him. "I'm afraid."

"You don't need to be." His voice whispered in her ear. "Believe." His image faded completely away, and she was sucked back into the abyss.

Grace was bereft — her body drained. Just when she didn't think she could bear to stay in the sweat lodge for another minute, Mr. Stonecalfe thanked the spirits, and the ceremony was over.

The two women crawled out of the lodge, where they were helped to their feet by the fire keeper. Weak in spirit as well as body, Grace stumbled toward the river bank unable to speak. She found a place to sit on a flat rock and slipped her feet into the water.

Why had she ever agreed to do this? It was too much. Had her longing for another glimpse of her husband's face conjured him up in her mind? It had felt so real. She had smelled the citrus and amber scents of his cologne and felt his living breathing body close to hers, as he held her. She was so confused and disoriented by all of this.

She slid the rest of the way into the water, not only to clear the fog from her brain, but to cleanse her body from the effects of the sweat. When she felt able, she walked over to join Mary and Mr. Stonecalfe who were talking quietly by the fire. She was loath to interrupt them because she knew they were probably talking about Mary's vision. She needn't have worried. Upon seeing Grace out of the corner of her eye, Mary waved her over to join them.

Mary took Grace's river-cooled hands into her own. "How do you feel?"

"I'm not sure. I feel better after my swim, but I haven't been able to make any sense out of the experience."

"Do not despair. Healing is a process that continues long after the sweat is complete. Would you like to share your vision?" Mr. Stonecalfe asked.

"There's not much to tell really. I saw my husband, Charles, and he kept telling me I wasn't alone and that I should believe."

"This is possible. Sometimes the spirit of the deceased chooses to stay close."

"If he's still supposed to be here, why can't I see him?"

"When those we love die, they are only dead to our eyes. They go on to live in another form. Remember that all of life is unified and sacred. What you experienced in the spirit world is somehow connected to the present. Now that you have exposed your wounds to the Great Spirit, the answer will be revealed to you when the time is right. When it comes to the realms of the spirit world, nothing is left to chance," Mr. Stonecalfe assured her.

"I was hoping you'd be able to clear things up for me right away," Grace said.

"I can only assist you in finding the answer within yourself, for that is surely where it lies."

She would have to trust that what Mr. Stonecalfe said was true: that all things would be revealed to her in time.

The evening ended with a shared meal around the camp fire. "Did you find what you were looking for in your vision?" Grace inquired of Mary.

I did," Mary smiled.

"Well, are you going to tell me?" she teased lightly.

Mary placed her metal plate on the ground and wiped her hands on her shorts, while she gathered her thoughts. "I have come to understand, that the man I married hasn't existed for a long time. I just didn't want to accept it."

"What do you mean?"

"You already know that when Bill died, David couldn't forgive himself. I thought maybe he just needed some time and eventually things would go back to the way they were. That was foolish. We were both changed by the war."

Grace waited for her to elaborate.

"While David was fighting in France, I had to manage without him. It changed my view of the world. Maybe not in the same way the war changed his, but changed nonetheless. Maybe it was asking too much for us to ever make a go of it again. Too much had happened."

"Are you saying that you and David grew apart?"

"Yes. I think I was holding on to the dream of what we had when we were first married. That part of our lives was over. It had been for a long time. I just couldn't see it. At least now I know that my husband is finally at peace," Mary said.

"What makes you say that?" Grace asked.

Mary gave her friend a mysterious smile. "I just know."

Grace watched Mary's eyes fill with light. "Now I'm really curious."

Mary tried to formulate the words. "I don't know how to describe it. One minute I was rooted to the earth, the next I was lifted..."

Grace nodded, recognizing her own sense of lightness right before she met Charles in her vision.

"My body felt weightless, as I soared through the silky clouds, and the dreamy blue sky. Up and up I went, travelling faster and faster. But it didn't feel fast, you know what I mean?" She glanced at Grace who nodded. "It felt like I was floating to a place where there was no sense of time. Then I saw millions of stars clustered together. They were so close, it created a pathway across the sky, and I was on it. When I looked back, I could see Turtle Island, all green and blue, through a scattering of white clouds. Earth looked so beautiful suspended in the middle of space like that."

Grace sat forward in her seat. It was so different from her own experience yet similar in some ways. When she glanced over at Mr. Stonecalfe, she noticed that he had this faraway look in his eyes. It was as though he knew exactly what Mary was talking about — had been to this place himself. She waited, but it seemed that Mary was done speaking.

"And then what happened?" Grace finally asked when it seemed that there was no more forthcoming.

Mary looked surprised at the question. "That's it."

"I thought you'd see David or something."

"I didn't need to," she said.

Grace shook her head in confusion.

"Understanding came to me by just being there."

"If you didn't talk to anyone, how did you come to an understanding?"

Mary took Grace by the hand and smiled. "There are other ways to communicate in the Spirit World."

"Oh," Grace said, as though she understood.

Seeing her puzzlement, Mary continued. "All I know is I went to visit Sky World and experienced peace in the House of Souls."

"Where David is?" Grace asked to clarify her understanding.

"And you are at peace also," Mr. Stonecalfe said.

Mary smiled and nodded.

* * * * * *

The fire crackled and popped, and smoke climbed into the heavens, but all of this went unnoticed by the trio, as their thoughts remained connected to Sky World. Animals skittered about, and the river continued to silently shift, as it had done for eons. Out of this sacred space, Mary's hushed voice bid Mr. Stonecalfe an indulgence. "Would you tell the story of the *Seven Fires Prophecy?*"

"It is a night for dreaming," Mr. Stonecalfe said after careful consideration. "I will be happy to share this story with you. Would you like to hear it?" he asked Grace.

"I would love to hear the story of your people."

"It is the story for all people," he gently corrected.

Mr. Stonecalfe's voice reverberated in the mystical night, as he began to tell the migration story of the Ojibwe nation, from Eastern Canada, to the land of the Great Lakes.

"It is said, that *The Prophesy of the Seven Fires* came into being thousands of years ago and continues to this day. The prophet of the First Fire counselled the Anishinaabeg to move inland, from the Eastern shores of North America, to protect the Ojibwe sacred teachings of the Midewiwin Lodge. Many did not want to go, because life was good for them there. But they were warned, that if they did not follow the prophecy, all would be destroyed. They were told that there would be seven stopping places along the way. They would know the right place to stop, when they came to a place where food grows on water. It is believed that they were referring to the wild rice that grows in abundance around the Great Lakes.

"During the time of the Second Fire, the Sacred Megis was lost. This shell is sacred to the Mediwiwin Lodge, as it is infused with the power to pass on the secrets of the Mediwiwin to the Anishinaabeg. When it was lost, the power of the Midewiwin diminished also. But all was not completely lost. A boy was born to show them the way back to their traditional ways. Once again, they were led by the Sacred Megis, and the People flourished. There was food for everyone.

"During the time of the Third Fire, there was cultural and spiritual growth. They were happy. Their ceremonies and songs were regenerated. But still they searched, for the prophecy foretold of a land where food grows on water. At this time, the people split and went in different directions. But they met up again many years later, at a place where the sacred shell rose from the waters.

"At the time of the Fourth Fire, two prophets came to the People and told them of the coming of the light-skinned race. The first prophet told them that if the light-skinned race wears the face of brotherhood, they would join together and learn from each other and become one mighty nation. This new nation would join with two other nations, to create the mightiest nation of all. These four nations, as you may have guessed, are the white man, the red man, the black man, and the yellow man.

"The second prophet warned them that if the light-skinned race comes carrying weapons, and their hearts are filled with greed for the riches of the land, they cannot be trusted. They must prove themselves as brothers.

"There was a great struggle during the time of the Fifth Fire. With the coming of the white man, there was the threat of the people abandoning the old ways in favour of Christianity, and the system of barter brought by the fur traders and merchants. The People believed they could embrace these new ways without damaging their culture. The light skinned race tried to destroy the People and take away their way of life.

"The prophet of the Sixth Fire told the People that once the ways of the light-skinned race were adopted, it would mean the end of the old ways. Their children would be taken away from their families to go to special schools. There, they would be forced to learn to live as white men. This would mean that the elders would lose their reason for living.

"Many of the People did not believe these dire predictions. They were the ones to suffer the most. But when the predictions came true, a group of visionaries knew that in order to protect the Midewiwin way of life, they must gather all the scrolls that record the ceremonies. These scrolls were placed in a hollow log, and buried in a hole dug out of the side of a cliff, until the people could safely practice their religion without fear.

"In the time of the Seventh Fire, a prophet with a strange light in his eyes said that New People would emerge to retrace their steps and find what was left by the trail. They knew this would not be easy. If the New People remained strong, the Midewiwin Lodge would rise again.

"When this happens, the light-skinned race will have to choose between the road of technology, and the road of the Spirit. If they choose the right road, the Seventh Fire will light the Eighth and final fire, of peace, love, and brotherhood. If they choose the road of technology, it could mean the destruction of all the people of the Earth.

"So you see, the prophecy speaks to all the nations to work together to protect the land, air, and the water, which was given to us in keeping by the Great Spirit, instead of continuing on its current path of destruction.

As Grace stared into the flickering flames, she was acutely aware that something extraordinary had occurred. Her eyes had been opened to a larger vision of the world. Her mind drifted back to October of the previous year, when the world came so close to extinction, during the Cuban Missile Crisis. She would never forget those thirteen days while everyone waited, with fear in their hearts, for the outcome. Who would have thought that after surviving such a horrendous catastrophe, her husband would die of a heart attack a mere five months later?

Grace lay back on the blanket and stared up at the night sky. She saw the cluster of stars that Mary spoke of in her vision. From where she lay, the Milky Way looked like it was separate from Earth. In reality, Earth was part of the Milky Way, in the same way the people of the world were part of one mighty nation, which Mr. Stonecalfe spoke of in his prophesy.

* * * * * *

Despite the lateness of the previous evening, Grace awakened early the following morning. It was the perfect opportunity to watch the sun come up. She wrapped a quilt around her nightgown and slipped on her canvas shoes. Coffee in hand, she stepped gingerly along the rocky ground, to where the Adirondack chairs overlooked Dry Pine Bay. She folded the quilt securely around her legs, inhaled the acidic flavour of her coffee, and waited.

It wasn't long before the sun split through the pines opposite Dry Pine Bay and cast golden stripes on the umbral morning. When the sun reached the crest of the trees, the surrounding sky turned red and gold and reflected off the surface of the river in waves. The sight brought tears to her eyes and stirred up feelings concerning her vision of the previous day. She pulled out her journal from beneath the quilt and contemplated how to begin.

Dear Charles: July 1, 1963

As you know by now, I went through with the sweat lodge ceremony – after all, you were there too, weren't you? I'm still not sure what was real and what wasn't. It certainly felt real to have your arms around me again. I didn't want to come back. But as far I can tell, something did happen, so I'll go with that.

I wish you could have been clear in your message to me. But these mystical meetings tend to be that way, don't they? I guess it's up to me to figure out what you meant when you said not to be afraid, because I'm never alone. Well, I certainly wasn't alone in that moment, was I? At least I don't think I was. But what of now? Now I am alone – alone and afraid of what the future holds. How does one overcome that fear?

Grace paused in her writing to gaze across the water. Her quilt slid from her shoulders, and she let it. The air was warming up now, and she wanted to feel the sun caress her skin.

When I think back to the fearful days of the Cuban Missile Crisis, I realize that danger is an intrinsic part of life. Rather than being frightened by that possibility, I find it oddly comforting. It means there's no point in pretending that life is all good. Bad things happen to everyone. At the same time, I'm not used to giving up control. The question is, can I learn to accept that things are out of my hands? Is this where faith comes in? But faith in what? Faith in God? Faith in the world? Faith in myself? Mr. Stonecalfe said I needed to have faith. But how can I have faith, when my world has been turned upside down?

During the sweat, I remember hearing a voice say, "The self must change as it goes through its life stages." But how must I change? Obviously I need to have faith in myself, but how do I do that when the world I knew is gone? I just can't magically conjure faith. There's that word again — faith. It seems like such a Christian word to be used for a Native ceremony. Yet, Mr. Stonecalfe used it many times. Is that the Christian part of himself coming out, or is faith something that crosses all religions? Of course it is. Faith is a fundamental part of our belief in something greater than ourselves. Now that I think about it, even the sweat ceremony had a sacredness to it. Things were blessed, prayers were said in the form of chants, and the smudging was just like the incense used in the Catholic Church. They're both used as a purification ritual. The smoke from the incense symbolized prayers drifting up to heaven, just like the smoke from the pipe.

So, what do you think Charles? Do you think I'm being drawn back into my own religion, or am I getting wrapped up in the Native one? And does it really matter, so long as I have something to believe in?

Grace.

Grace placed her pen between the pages of her journal and closed it. The day was warming up. She tugged the quilt from around her legs, so she could feel the heat from the sun rays stroke her limbs, where they peeked out below her nightgown. She stretched her arms above her head to get the kinks out. She was ready for the new day.

XIV

Grace couldn't put it off any longer. She needed groceries. So the day after Canada day, she made a list and headed for the Trading Post. She tried to ignore Mr. Franco as much as possible, but when it came time to pay for her items, she was met with his hostile glare.

"I heard tell you've been dealing in sorcery," he growled.

"How did you hear about...?"

"When people get up to no good, word gets around," he sneered.

"Excuse me?"

"You heard me. I thought I told you to stay away from them Indians. Everyone around here knows you took part in one of their voodoo ceremonies."

"You have no right..."

"Everyone knows them Indian ceremonies conjure bad spirits." He pointed his fat finger in her face. "I'm telling you sister, if them bad spirits stir up trouble, we'll know who to blame."

Heart racing, Grace straightened her backbone and said, "I don't think that's any of your business who I spent my time with, or what I do." She picked up her things and marched out the door.

"You mark my words, you'll regret the day you took up with them Indians," he growled after her.

Grace hurried along the hard-packed ground toward the marina and her boat. She maneuvered her small craft through the channel, let out the throttle, and pointed toward home. She raced across the bay in a blur of tears and almost ran into the dock. But she managed to control the boat enough that the dock only pitched and swayed, as she came to a jarring stop. She secured the boat and abandoned her groceries on the deck. She needed to walk.

Grace hiked over the rocky ground and fumed. How had Franco found out about the sweat so quickly? It only happened Sunday night. Her thoughts were so scattered, she didn't see the dip in the rock. She stumbled and almost fell. She berated herself. Why did she let Mr. Franco upset her all the time? She resolved to pay better attention to the ground beneath her feet. But this only served to make her unaware of her surroundings and she lost her bearings.

She surveyed the landscape. Nothing seemed familiar. There were no markings on the rock face, and the occasional vegetation looked untouched by human passage. Her heart hammered in her breast. She had to remain calm. She looked this way and that, but the panic was making it difficult for her to think. Why hadn't she paid better attention? "Oh my God, what am I going to do?" she whispered. Pupils dilated with fear, she scurried about like a rabbit in a warren — first one way, and then another — trying to find the way back. She broke out in a cold sweat. A sob hiccupped in her throat, but she forced it back. "Damn that Henry Franco anyway," she blasted. "You're not going to win this one." With that thought in mind, she ceased all movement. With trembling lips, she closed her eyes and took a couple of deep breaths to calm her mind.

Once the pounding in her ears settled to a dull thud, she heard singing in the distance. How strangely comforting. It beckoned to her. With hope in her heart, she followed the melody all the way to the river, where it ceased. She chose not to question her good fortune. All she knew was that if she followed the river in the general direction she'd come from, she'd make it home.

Torn between trying not to hurry for fear of falling, and the desire to return to the safety of her cabin, Grace made her way back along the river bank. When the terrain started to look familiar, she was able to breathe more steadily. Everything would be all right. What a relief it was when she stepped through the copse of trees that led to her camp. But just as suddenly her heart stopped, when she discovered a man wandering around the camp.

"Grace, is that you?" the apparition called out.

Relief washed over her, as she recognized George Watson's voice. She hurried toward him.

"Is everything all right?" he asked upon her approach. "I saw your bag of groceries on the deck and was worried."

"I got lost while I was out walking," she said.

"Well, I'm glad you managed to find your way back."

She gave him a weak smile. "I followed the river."

"Well, you're safe now."

George's soothing words triggered an unexpected reaction in Grace. She threw her arms around George and cried. "I was so scared. I thought I was going to be stuck outside all night."

George stumbled slightly, braced his legs, and patted her back awkwardly.

At the sound of a passing motor boat, Grace pulled away. "I'm so embarrassed."

"There's no need to be." George stepped back and coughed.

"What are you doing here?" she thought to ask.

"Never mind that now," he said. "Why don't we get you inside, and I'll make us some coffee."

Grace wiped her eyes. "Oh dear, I seem to have lost my manners."

"You're upset." George picked up the packages and followed Grace through the front door.

Still shaken from her ordeal, it took Grace a moment to remember where she kept the coffee canister. As she passed it to him, she suddenly realized that she was alone with a man whom she really didn't know all that well. She moved to the other side of the room to put some distance between them. At least then, she could claim a modicum of propriety between them. She didn't want him to get the wrong idea.

"Feel better now?" George asked when they finished their coffee.

"I do feel more alert. That coffee was pretty strong."

"Sorry. Now you know why I spend so much time at the diner."

"But you offered to make it."

"I said I would make it, not that it would be good."

Grace chuckled and relaxed a bit. "So, are you going to tell me why wanted to see me?"

Recalling himself, George picked up a package off the table. "I thought you might be interested in this book."

"That was very thoughtful of you, but I could have picked it up next time you're in the diner."

"When you take a look at it, you'll understand why I didn't want to wait." He carefully unwrapped the package and slid it across the table toward her.

"What's so special about this book that it couldn't wait?" She glanced at it without really seeing it.

"Well, it's not a book in the traditional sense. There's very little written information about the voyageurs, as many of them couldn't write. But I did manage to locate this diary, written by Samuel de Champlain himself, dating back to 1615. Though I was only able to get a copy of the original, he does talk about his time with the Natives and his desire to forge a fur-trading partnership with them."

Grace's interest was piqued. She accepted the book and placed it carefully on the table. "May I?" she asked and reverently smoothed her hands over the cover. "I only wish Charles were here to share this with me."

"Charles was your husband?"

"Yes. He was a History Professor at the University of Toronto." She carefully turned the pages. "Oh my. I know it's only a copy but, I feel like Champlain just stepped into the room."

"Now you know how I feel."

"Thank you for sharing this with me," she smiled.

"I knew you'd appreciate its significance," he said, as he watched her turn to the pages.

"Have you read it?" Grace asked.

"Every word."

"Tell me what you know."

George thought for a moment before a light came into his eyes. "Did you know that Champlain once got lost in the woods?"

"You're just saying that to make me feel better."

"It's true. He was hunting with the Huron Indians, when he got separated from the group while in pursuit of an unusual species of bird. It took him three days to find his way back." He folded his meaty hands across his ample stomach.

"How did he find his way back?"

"He followed the river."

"Now I know you're teasing. That's exactly what I did."

"Scouts honour," he said placing his index, middle and ring fingers together in the Boy Scout salute. "In fact, you might be interested to know that he was also a cartographer."

"Now I don't feel so bad."

"You're certainly in good company." He leaned past her and turned the pages until he found what he was looking for. "In fact, this is a map of Quebec and Ontario drawn by Champlain."

Grace admired the details. "Oh my. It looks quite accurate doesn't it? Look, there's the St. Lawrence Seaway. And isn't that the Great Lakes?"

"And what about this one?" George picked out a picture this time. "This is a sketch of the defeat of the Iroquois."

Grace studied the drawing. "That must be Champlain there." She pointed to the drawing of a man who stood between opposing forces armed with an Arquebus, while arrows flew over his head. "Who were the rival forces?" Grace asked.

"Champlain was fighting alongside the Algonquin against the Iroquois," he replied.

Grace placed a hand over her mouth and yawned. "Excuse me."

"I'm boring you," George noted.

"Not at all. I've enjoyed hearing all about Champlain. He's fascinating. It's just that it's been a long day," she shrugged.

He accepted her comment with good grace and got up to leave.

"Don't forget this." Grace handed the diary back to him.

George carefully wrapped the diary in a soft cloth and headed for the door. Before leaving, he said, "It's such a pleasure to talk with someone who enjoys history as much as I do."

"It's my pleasure entirely," she assured him.

There was a long pause before he spoke.

"What is it?" Grace asked.

"It's nothing."

"It's not nothing. What did you want to say?"

"I just wondered whether you'd like to stop by the library some time to look at it more thoroughly." He indicated the diary with a quick pass.

"That sounds lovely," she smiled.

He let out a breath and said good night.

Grace watched George leave through the picture window. He was adept with his motor boat in ways he seemed to lack on dry land, she noted with a smile. She liked him immensely. But, she reminded herself, she'd save herself a lot of trouble if she didn't get too close to him.

She turned out the overhead lights and got ready for bed. Once settled, she placed her journal on her upturned knees and began to write.

Dear Charles: July 2, 1963

That Henry Franco has been causing trouble for me again. It appears that he took exception to my becoming involved in the sweat ceremony. Why does he care so much? I

*personally can't regret it, as it brought us together again
— if only for a moment. I'd do it all again despite his disapproval. But I can't deny it. His words upset me to the point
that I got lost in the woods because I was blinded by anger.
I know I give that man far too much control. He just has
a way of unnerving me. I was ever so glad when I made
it back to camp and found George Watson waiting for me
and not Henry Franco, as I first feared. I'm afraid I acted
inappropriately and threw myself at him. I just needed to
feel safe for a moment. I think I embarrassed the poor man.*

*I hope you won't be upset if I admit how much I enjoy
George's company. He is, after all, a lover of history, just
like you. I do miss our discussions about such things.
Conversations at my book club usually revolved around
talk of child care and other mundane aspects of wifely
endeavours. I know I need to be careful lest people get the
wrong idea about George and me. I don't know why it's so
hard for people to believe that a man and a woman can be
nothing more than friends? Please understand that I have
no feelings for him beyond friendship and a co-conspirator
in history. I miss you terribly, and while I am at times
lonely without you, I have no wish to entangle myself with
another man. So why, I wonder, do I feel so guilty?*

Grace.

XV

The morning sun shone in her eyes. She could feel the heat it generated on her face. She tried to think. Then she remembered the events of the previous night and groaned. She rolled out of bed and shuffled to the bathroom.

While brushing her teeth, Grace caught sight of her reflection in the mirror. She leaned forward to get a closer look at the spidery red lines that fanned out from her pupils. She spit in the sink and rinsed.

She took her morning coffee down to the river. It was the beginning of a new day. There was still a chance to find some peace in the beauty that surrounded her. A hump back rock, bleached white and foliated with bluish-grey, emerged out of a landscape dotted with patches of green scrub. Pine trees thrived in the sparse environment, some in clusters, while others stood as lonely sentinels along the riverbank.

Grace knew that George was expecting her to come to town to see the diaries again. And she was happy to do so at some point. But for the moment, she was afraid to run into Mr. Franco again. She wasn't ready to face him yet. She knew she was being a coward, but there it was.

She decided to go for a walk, to help get her mind off things, paying special attention to her surroundings. It wasn't long before she ran into Maggie.

"No need to sneak up Grace, I can hear you coming a mile away." Maggie wiped her paint brush on an old cloth.

"Am I that noisy?" A tree branch snapped beneath her feet. She blushed.

"It's not easy to be quiet with all this debris on the ground," Maggie offered.

Grace sat on a fallen log. "You're so lucky to be able to come here every summer."

"You can too — now."

"I thought that might be true once, but now I'm not so sure."

Maggie sat down beside her friend. "Oh, what's happened to change your mind?"

"Oh nothing really. It's just that sometimes I don't feel like I belong here."

"If not here, then where?"

Grace thought about what awaited her back in Toronto. Charles was gone and so were the friendships she thought were hers. "Well I don't really know any more. But not here."

"Look, the only place you need to feel like you belong is right here," Maggie said thumping her chest with two fingers.

"Maybe you're right," Grace replied with little enthusiasm.

"Of course I'm right. I'm always right. Ask Albert."

"Albert wouldn't dare disagree with you," Grace chuckled.

"Albert's a smart man. He knows what's what. Come on. I need a cup of coffee."

It wasn't long before the two women sat across from each other at Maggie's kitchen table, where Grace told Maggie about the sweat ceremony.

"You don't sound like someone who doesn't belong here," Maggie pointed out, when Grace finished telling her story. "You had the courage to embrace something totally out of your realm of experience. So what's happened since the day of the sweat that makes you think you don't belong here?"

Grace watched while a fly buzzed around the toast crumbs left on the table from breakfast. "Maybe I just changed my mind about this place."

Maggie picked up a discarded newspaper, rolled it tightly, and swatted the pesky fly. "You can try that tack with other people, honey." She picked up the dead fly and tossed it out the door. "But this is me you're talking to. Out with it," she continued and sat back down.

"Maggie, what do you really think about Native rituals?" Grace said at last.

"So that's it." She rolled back the sleeves of her white shirt. "Has somebody been giving you a hard time about that sweat?"

"You didn't answer my question," Grace pointed out.

"Well, for what it's worth, there's all kinds of belief systems in this world. I have no right to pass judgement."

"I wish everyone was so open-minded about things they don't understand," Grace said.

The gurgling percolator demanded Maggie's attention. While Grace waited, she looked around the kitchen with its open shelves full of the milky green Jadite dishes first made popular in the 1930s. Rows of neatly lined plates, bowls, and mugs sat beside gleaming glassware. Curtains covered the shelves beneath the counter where Maggie presumably kept those items not pretty enough for display.

Maggie returned to the table, filled both coffee cups, and placed the percolator on the Formica table top. "Someone has said something."

Grace took a sip of the hot liquid before speaking. "When I went into the Trading Post yesterday to pick up a few things, Mr. Franco accused me of taking part in voodoo ceremonies." She took a deep quivering breath. "He said that it would bring evil spirits — that I would be to blame if something bad happened."

"Oh dear."

"What do you know of Mr. Franco's history?" Grace asked, in the hope she'd gain some insight into the man.

"Well, let me see," Maggie said, as she searched her memory. "Henry was born late in life to Ruth and Edgar Franco. A bit of a surprise if you will. I'm afraid they were ill equipped to handle a new baby set in their ways as they were. Afraid he was just too much for them, especially when he grew up. He always did what he pleased — used to getting his own way. He was different with Sarah — happier. I guess love can change even the most recalcitrant of people." She shrugged. "Until she said no to his offer of marriage. Well, not Sarah exactly, but her parents weren't happy about the union."

"Maybe if Sarah had agreed to marry him, he might be different now. As it is, I just want to slap him, he makes me so angry."

"That's not exactly ladylike. Besides, it would only have made things worse."

"I'm tired of being a lady if it means I can't even defend myself."

"You shouldn't have to defend yourself. Look, it doesn't take much to figure out. Henry Franco has always had it in for the Native people. You just got caught in the middle."

"I can understand why Mr. Franco was upset because Sarah ran off with Joseph Crow all those years ago. I just assumed he'd be over it by now."

"The only person he ever really loved was Sarah, and she didn't seem to care enough to fight for him. The life he lived with Bertha was content enough, but I don't think he was ever really happy."

"But now he's taking his unhappiness out on me."

"I will tell you this: Henry's just full of bluster. I don't think you have anything to worry about, so you mustn't let him get the better of you."

When Albert came in from his wanderings, Maggie burst out with, "Did you know that Henry Franco has been giving our Grace a hard time?"

"Is that so?" Albert said calmly. His gaze wandered from one woman to the other.

"Maggie please..."

"Albert and I have no secrets from each other."

Maggie filled Albert in on the details of their conversation that ended with, "I told her she has nothing to worry about with Henry Franco."

"I'm inclined to agree with Mother," Albert said. "He's full of swagger, that's all."

"Do you really think so?"

Albert patted her hand. "I'm sure of it."

Albert's words helped to settle Grace's mind, at least for the time being. But later that night, when the doors were locked and the lights turned off, she couldn't block out the image of Mr. Franco's angry face.

XVI

Grace decided it was time she went to Sunday Service at the local church. What better way to face Mr. Franco, if he was indeed there, than in a church surrounded by other people? In this way, she could at least give the affectation of bravery. When she walked down the center aisle to sit with Mary and the boys, she sensed someone was watching her. She searched the attendants and found him sitting near the back. The sneer on his face was enough to give pause to even the most stalwart of hearts. Steadfast in her resolve to stay, she sat rigidly before the altar.

Oddly, it had taken a Native ceremony to remind Grace that despite the fact that she had turned away from God, He hadn't turned away from her. The night she got lost, some otherworldly power had shown her the way. Whether it was inside a church, or a sweat lodge; whether she called it God, or the Great Spirit, there was no denying that there was something greater at work in the world. Grace decided to stop turning away and to embrace, not just the teachings of the church, but the teachings of all things spiritual.

After the service, George came over to let her know that there was a request from another library for the Champlain diaries. He would only have them for a few more days.

"I have to work tomorrow, but I could come the day after that. How would that be?" she offered.

"It may take some time to go over them. You don't want to be rushed," he pointed out.

"Of course," she said, wondering how best to solve her dilemma.

"Why don't you stop by this afternoon?" George suggested.

"But the library is closed on a Sunday. I'm not sure that would be appropriate." But when Grace's eyes locked with Henry Franco, his cold distain written plainly on his face, she changed her mind. "This afternoon would be fine."

* * * * * *

"I knew Champlain would have to travel down the French River to get to Georgian Bay, but to actually see it written in his own hand brings it alive somehow," Grace said to George later that afternoon.

"Yes, he travelled the French River many times over the years and met many diverse tribes along the way."

"Just imagine, a piece of Canadian history took place right on our doorstep."

"It is quite remarkable, isn't it?"

Sometime later, Grace blurted out, "This is amazing."

"What's that?" George asked.

"It says here, that between April 24, 1615 and August 17, of the same year, Champlain travelled from the palaces of France to the pioneer town of Tadoussac, Quebec. Then by August, he was living with the Huron Indians. Isn't it remarkable that they could travel such great distances so quickly during that time period?" Grace pointed out.

"I don't know about the French sailing ships, but I do know the voyageurs were able to travel great distances in a short period of time. They worked long hard hours, paddling their canoes with only short breaks, while they navigated the river. There wasn't much food, and the working conditions were primitive. On top of that, there was the added need to adjust to the cultural differences of the various tribes. Why, just between Quebec and Georgian Bay alone, they had to learn to deal with the Huron, the Nipissing, the Iroquois, the Ottawa, and the Algonquian. Although some of the voyageurs only worked for short periods of time so they could make money to invest in their farms and support their families, there were many who made it their life's work."

"It must have been a hard life."

George tilted his head, and closed one eye, deep in thought. "I don't think they thought of it in terms of hard or easy. I think they just did whatever was necessary to survive. If they wanted to be successful while trading with the Natives, they needed to be able to understand their ways. That's why Champlain sent Étienne Brûlé to live with the Huron: so that he could learn all about them and report back to him. He knew that it was important in order to have good trade relations."

"I recall you said that Champlain lived with the Huron as well?"

"That's right. After he was shot in the leg with an arrow, during a raid on the Iroquois, Champlain spent the winter of 1615-16 living with them. Darontal, the chief of the Huron tribe, told him that it would be too dangerous to return to Quebec and encouraged him to spend the winter with them while his wounds healed. While he was there, he kept a record of how they lived."

"I imagine living with the Huron would make a person more accepting of others."

George considered this before replying. "It's hard to say. On the one hand, Champlain was instrumental in bringing Jesuit priests from France to convert the local tribes. That does suggest that he felt they were heathens in need of civilizing. On the other hand, he did have a good relationship with them. That may have been due to necessity. The Natives knew the area that Champlain wanted to explore. It seems politic to get along."

"You have a point there," Grace considered. "What I can't understand, is why the Natives accepted Christianity, when it was predicted that the coming of the white-man would bring their downfall."

"Did you learn about that from your reading?"

"No, Mr. Stonecalfe told me about the *Seven Fires Prophecy*."

George nodded. "Unfortunately, the Natives never stood a chance in the face of the white man's idea of progress. But it wasn't religion that was the problem. It had more to do with Colonialism. The Colonists believed that their way was better than the Natives."

The couple studied and talked throughout the afternoon, until Grace leaned back in her chair to stretch.

"We've been at this for a long time. What do you say we give it a break?" George suggested.

Grace checked the time on the wall clock. "I don't know. I should probably get on home to make dinner. I was so engrossed in all this, I lost track of the time."

"You could always stay here and eat. There's not much point in both of us eating alone."

When Grace reluctantly walked through the living room, she noticed it had an untouched look about it — like no one had used it since his wife, Ruth, left to visit their daughter in Sudbury. The kitchen, on the other hand, was another matter. Chaos reigned wherever her eyes rested. An open jar of peanut butter sat on the table with a knife sticking out of it. And the strawberry jam was rimmed with peanut butter. Apparently, he felt one utensil was good enough for both. A coffee cup and plate had been left on the table amidst a scattering of crumbs, probably because there was no room in the sink from the look of things.

"Excuse the mess," George shrugged. "I forget to clean up after myself sometimes."

Grace started to clear the table. "How can you have so many dishes when you always eat at the diner?"

"You forget that Mary doesn't stay open for dinner."

"So you cook dinner for yourself?"

He picked up a dirty frying pan off the stove. "I can manage to make a grilled cheese or fry up a mess of eggs."

"At least let me wash that first." She took the frying pan from him, and made some room in the sink, so she could wash it.

George got some cheese out of the fridge and carried it to the counter. He cleared a space to butter some bread and add the cheese. This, he placed in the newly washed frying pan. While he waited for the pan to heat up, he reached past Grace to turn on the radio. The romantic chords of Johnny Mathis crooning *Chances Are* drifted out of the box creating an atmosphere of intimacy. Grace kept her head down while she washed and stacked the dishes in a rack to dry. She was beginning to think she should have gone directly home. To fill the silence, and to remind them both that this was strictly business, Grace asked, "When do you expect your wife back home?"

George flipped the grilled cheese in the pan. "Whenever she can tear herself away from our new grandchild."

"Why didn't you go with her?"

"I was there when he was born. Besides, I was only in the way there. I'd rather be here working."

"You miss your wife?"

"Every day."

Grace relaxed. "I remember when my first grandchild was born. Well, my only grandchild really. A little girl named after me. As you can imagine, after two boys, I longed for a little girl. I love her to death. I just wish she lived closer, so I could see more of her."

"Where is she?" George reached into the fridge and brought out the milk and ketchup and put them on the freshly washed table. "We'll need glasses," he muttered to himself and searched through the empty cupboard, where he found two mismatched plastic goblets.

"In Alberta. My son teaches there. He seems to like it, so I don't expect he will ever come back to Ontario."

"What about your other son?"

"Jack? He has his own business. He's always been good with cars and has never wanted to do anything but fix them. Charles was upset at first. He wanted both the boys to get a university education. But Jack is strong-willed, just like his grandmother, and was determined to do what he wanted."

"Is he happy?" George placed a piping hot sandwich on a plate and cut it in half. "You eat this while I make another," he said.

"I think so." Grace took a bite out of the sandwich. "Mmmm, this is so good," she said as she scooped up the trail of cheese from her mouth to the bread and licked her fingers.

"Then, that's all you can ask for, isn't it?" He poured them both a glass of milk and joined her at the table.

"You're right of course."

A knock at the kitchen door startled them. Grace placed her sandwich back on the plate, wiped her hands on her shorts, and waited while George answered it.

"Oh, Alice. Hello. I wasn't expecting to see you today." George stepped aside to let the woman enter.

The scent of cinnamon and apple filled the air, when she stepped into the room. "I just took some apple pies out of the oven and thought you'd like one," she said as she placed the pie on the kitchen table. "Oh." She hesitated. "I didn't know you had company."

"Grace, this is my sister-in-law, Alice Frye. Alice, this is Grace Irwin. She just came over to look at some historical documents."

"Is that so?" Alice stared at the table set for two.

"We were just having a quick bite before Grace left. No point in eating alone, don't you know. Would you care to join us?"

"Um, no, I don't think so. Harold is waiting for his supper." There was a momentary silence before Alice said, "Well, I'd better be going." She gave Grace a perfunctory nod on her way out the door.

"I think it's time for me to go," Grace said and prepared to leave.

"You don't need to do that. We've done nothing wrong."

"That's not what your sister-in-law thinks."

"At least finish your supper," he said.

"Under the circumstances, I think it's best that I leave right away, don't you?"

George flushed. "I suppose you're right."

Grace wanted to kick herself for going against her better judgment. What was she thinking spending a Sunday afternoon with a married man? Damn that Henry Franco anyway. If it wasn't for his imperious presence at church, maybe she wouldn't have accepted George's invitation. But deep down, she knew it was her own fault for allowing him to get to the better of her.

She made another grilled cheese sandwich when she got home, since her dinner with George had been interrupted. She ate on the deck, in the hope that the soothing sounds of the river would relax her. She wish she'd thought to bring her journal outside, and she debated whether to go and get it. But she knew herself well enough to know that writing calmed her, so she picked up her dishes on her way inside to retrieve it.

Dear Charles: July 7, 1963

I know that spending time with a married man this afternoon was unconscionable. I just couldn't seem to help myself. When George suggested I come over to look at the Champlain diaries, I was planning to say no. I knew it wasn't appropriate. But when I saw Henry Franco's face, I wasn't about to let his disapproval influence me. But he did influence me, didn't he? I went to spite the man, and look what happened.

Things were fine, until George's sister-in-law turned up with a pie and found us together. It was obvious she didn't believe we were only working. I knew it was time to leave. I suppose I can't blame her. I'm sure, from her perspective, it looked bad. I just wanted to read the diaries before they had to be returned. Now someone else thinks I'm guilty of impropriety. Is my loneliness a threat to everyone around me? Damn.

Grace.

Grace thought about what she couldn't say in the journal. That moment of intimacy in the kitchen — the music, the close confines of the space, and the comfortable conversation. Well, relatively comfortable, if you didn't count the odd feeling of déjà vu she experienced with George. It reminded her of her life with Charles. The evenings in the kitchen after dinner. They talked about the events of the day and made plans for the weekend. Sometimes, Charles would take her in his arms, and they'd dance around the kitchen. One thing would lead to another — Grace shook her head. Somehow the two memories had become intertwined.

XVII

Grace's feet hurt, her back hurt, and she was starting to get a headache, from the heat of the diner. She trailed into the kitchen, which was even hotter, and inquired, "Is there any aspirin back here? I've got a splitting headache."

Mary flipped the sizzling burgers on the grill. "There should be some in the cupboard by the sink."

Grace popped two of the little white pills into her mouth and washed it down with a glass of cool water. "How can you stand the heat in here?"

Mary wiped her forehead with a nearby towel. "You get used to it."

"Well I hope I get used to it soon. The heat in here is unbearable." Grace stepped back through the swinging door, to where the lunch crowd waited.

"Hello dear."

The unexpected voice caught Grace off guard. "Mother!"

"It's nice to know that you haven't forgotten me completely."

"What are you doing here?"

"I might ask you the same question?"

Grace straightened to her full meagre height. "I work here."

"Order up," Mary called from the kitchen.

"I have to get that," Grace said, indicating the hamburger and fries under the warming lights.

"Surely someone else can take care of it."

"Everyone else is busy. Why don't you find a place to sit, and I'll bring you some coffee the first chance I get."

"Who's that?" Mary asked when Grace picked up the order.

"That's my mother."

"You don't seem very happy to see her."

Grace rubbed her temples. "I'm not."

"Uh-ho, like that is it?"

"You don't know the half of it."

"What are you gonna do?"

"The first chance I get, I'm going to find out why she's here."

"This is your last order. Go talk to her now," Mary said with a tilt of her head toward Grace's mother.

"Thanks." Grace delivered the hamburger and fries to table five, filled two coffee mugs, and went to sit with her mother. "So, Mother, to what do I owe this unexpected pleasure?"

"Does a mother need a reason to visit her daughter?"

"Well, this isn't exactly your style, is it Mother?" she said with a sweep of her hand.

"Whatever do you mean? When you were little, your father and I came to the French River all the time."

"And you hated it."

"Be that as it may, I was worried about you."

Grace softened a little. "Well, that's very nice of you Mother, but I'm doing just fine."

Her mother, Elizabeth, spoiled the little bit of good will Grace had, by saying, "That's not what I heard."

Grace sighed. "Dare I ask what you mean by that?"

"I just had a nice little chat with the gentleman at the Trading Post. A, what was his name again? Oh yes, a Mr. Frisco. He tells me, you've been doing all manner of inappropriate things. Let me see, what did he say? Oh yes, something about cavorting with a married man. And if that's not bad enough, he mentioned that you participated in a Native ritual. What would your father say?"

With every word Elizabeth spoke, the tension in Grace's head increased. It was bad enough that Mr. Franco was making her life difficult, why did her own mother have to take his side? She took a deep breath, afraid she'd say something she might regret. "First of all, his name is Franco, not Frisco. And secondly, Daddy probably would have joined me in the sweat lodge ceremony."

"Your father's tastes always were questionable."

"Daddy is open-minded," Grace pointed out.

"If you can call getting involved in heathen rituals being open-minded."

"Where is Daddy anyway?" Grace asked.

"I left him at home. I wanted to spend some time alone with my only child."

"How much time?"

Elizabeth wrung her hands, where they rested on her lap. "Long enough to satisfy myself that you're well."

"Is everything all right with you and Daddy?" Grace asked suddenly.

"Of course. Why would you ask such a thing?" she replied belligerently.

Grace paused, unsure whether or not to push her mother for more information.

"When will you be free to leave?" Elizabeth interrupted her thoughts.

"We still have to clear the tables and mop the floor, before I can go."

"So this is your ma." Mary presented a damp hand to the older woman.

"Mother, this is my good friend, Mary Whitefeather," Grace offered. "Mary, this is my mother, Elizabeth Moore."

"Mind if I call you Liz?" Mary asked, the devil in her eyes.

Elizabeth touched the tips of Mary's fingers. "If you don't mind, I prefer Elizabeth."

Mary tilted her head toward Grace and raised her eyebrows.

Grace's lips quivered, and the tension was momentarily eased.

Mary turned her attention back to Elizabeth. "You planning to stay long?"

"Not long," Elizabeth said vaguely.

"I really must get back to work, Mother," Grace said at last.

"That's OK kid. The girls and I can finish up here. I know you can't wait to spend some time with your ma." Mary waggled her eyebrows.

Grace glared at Mary, but Mary was unperturbed. She sashayed into the kitchen swinging her dish towel like a bawdy burlesque dancer.

Grace turned to her mother with a wan smile. "Let me just go and check my work schedule. I'll be right back."

"I'll get you for this," Grace said when she entered the kitchen and found Mary and Bob doubled over with laughter. No doubt she'd told Bob about Elizabeth.

"Is everything all right?" Elizabeth asked when Grace returned.

"Everything's fine Mother — just fine."

Elizabeth picked up the small overnight bag that sat next to her on the seat and handed it to Grace.

Grace accepted the burden with a sigh and led her mother to the marina.

Grace's head was pounding by the time they got home. After she helped her mother negotiate the floating dock and the stairs to the camp, she put her bags in the spare bedroom. "So what do you think of the place?" she asked.

"Very... rustic," Elizabeth offered.

Grace deliberately choose to misunderstand her mother's comment. "Thanks. I like it. Now, how about a glass of wine?"

"Oh, that would be lovely," she said with some relief. "It's nice to know that even in these back woods, you've managed to provide a bit of civilization."

"Whatever you say Mother." Grace mumbled under her breath and headed for the kitchen. She came back with two glasses of red wine and offered one to her mother. "Why don't we take our wine and sit by the river," Grace suggested.

"You mean walk back down that hill?"

"Of course, how foolish of me. Maybe we could sit on the deck instead?" Grace offered.

"I forgot how quiet it is here," Elizabeth said when they were settled.

"Well, it does takes some getting used to, that's for sure." Grace savoured the wine on her tongue before swallowing. She felt its heat course down her throat and settle in her stomach. The warm glow it created radiated through her body and helped her to relax. Her peace was to be short-lived, however.

"Now, about what Mr. Franco told me...?" Elizabeth said.

Grace was tired and hot after a day on her feet, and it made her snappish. "Before you start in on me, you need to know that anything Mr. Franco said will be tainted by his feelings toward me."

"And they are?"

"He hates me."

"Don't be ridiculous!" Elizabeth scoffed.

"It's true. He takes exception to my choice of friends."

"Can you blame him dear? It really isn't proper for you to be cavorting with those people."

"If you're referring to Mary Whitefeather, she -- and her sons, James and Will, have been good to me. Then there's the man who performed the sweat ceremony, Harry Stonecalfe."

"About that sweat ceremony. Do you really think that was appropriate?"

"If you must know, I was concerned at first. But after giving it a chance, I found it fascinating. Perhaps you could do the same."

"Humph! But really dear, you should associate with a better class of friends."

"Like the ones I had at home?"

"What's wrong with them?"

Grace sighed inwardly. Some things never changed. Whenever she was in the same room with her mother, she had to defend her choices. "After Charles died, they didn't want me around anymore. And if you really want to know the truth, I'm glad. We only became friends because they were the wives of Charles's colleagues.

"I'm afraid I don't understand. I met many of my dearest friends through your father."

"And I'm happy for you. However, I've come to realize that I don't belong with that crowd anymore."

"That may well be, but you don't belong with this one either."

Grace was exasperated. "You forget that I'm forty-seven years old. I can pick my own friends."

"You still have to consider your place in the world."

Grace rubbed the back of her neck. "And what is my place, Mother?"

"Something better than this, surely."

"But this is the best place I have ever known, Mother. I love it here." There were tears in Grace's eyes, as she recognized the truth of her own words.

Her mother saw it and relented. "You're just like your father."

"Thank you. That's the nicest thing you've ever said to me."

"Humph!" Elizabeth glared at the river.

Grace was glad for the silence. Her head was pounding abominably. To ensure her continued peace, Grace said, "Why don't you relax while I go and fix dinner."

"Don't be silly dear, I'll give you a hand."

As they sat across from each other at the kitchen table, Grace watched her mother eat. She really was quite out of place in these surroundings. She wore a silk blouse with a matching linen skirt on her matronly figure. Her coiffure, as always, was in perfect order. She was natural brunette, though years of colouring had turned it almost black. Grace knew she went to the beauty parlour every week, not only to get her hair done, but to pick up the latest gossip. Her mother was rarely seen without make-up and today was no exception. Her eyes were outlined in black, and she could see clumps of mascara on her lashes. Her cheeks were dots of red on a background of pale powder. And her once ruby lips were smudged from wiping them on her napkin.

"You know dear, despite what you might think of me, I do care about you."

Grace sighed and pushed her plate away. "I know you do Mother, but you have to trust me to take care of myself."

"I do trust you. It's just that you've never been on your own before."

"Now's as good as time as any to learn."

"And not making a very good job of it from what I hear."

"Can we talk please about something else now, Mother?"

"As you wish." Elizabeth took a deep breath. "So, how are you dear?"

"I'm fine Mother."

"What I mean is, how are you coping?"

Grace looked away for a moment before answering. "It's been hard at times, but I'm finding my way."

"Do you have any plans after you return home?"

"I'm not sure yet. That's something I'm trying to work out."

"It's a blessing Charles had a good insurance policy, so you don't have to work if you don't want to."

"You're right of course."

"I do wish you didn't have to work at the diner though."

"I should have known you'd get back to this."

"Honestly darling, sometimes I think you need to have a little faith in your mother."

"What do you mean?"

"I'm only trying to understand. If you are financially taken care of, why must you work at all?" she asked, palms up in entreaty.

"Because it gives me a sense of accomplishment."

"Surely you could get that from doing volunteer work."

"Now you sound just like Charles."

"Whatever do you mean?"

"He didn't understand my desire for employment either."

"I see. Perhaps you can explain it to me?"

Grace paused. "Being a wife and mother was wonderful in many ways. But there's more to me than that."

"Of course there is. But what do you expect to accomplish by working at the diner?"

"There's nothing wrong with working in a diner. I like the people I've met since I've been here. They're good, honest, hard-working people. I'd like to be more like them. Thank you, Mother. Until this moment, I didn't fully understand that myself. Now, if you have anything more to say to me, you can do it in the morning. I'm going to bed."

When Grace closed the bedroom door behind her, she was shaking. Altercations with her mother took so much out of her. It would be a long time before she slept.

XVIII

"I don't know why you didn't bring a pair of good walking shoes, Mother. You know how rocky the ground is around here." A glint of copper shone from a slot in her mother's penny loafers. They were on their way to visit Maggie. Grace thought it might ease the tension between the two of them to have a third person around.

"I wasn't planning on traipsing around the island," Elizabeth pointed out.

"But it's so pretty," Grace answered. "I can't imagine coming all this way and not taking the time to see the spectacular scenery."

"I just thought we'd confine ourselves to the village or the camp."

"Well, never mind, we're almost there." Grace shook her head. The two of them had been inseparable while she was growing up. As a child, she had enjoyed the attention, but when she got older and longed for more independence, her mother had a difficult time letting go of her only child.

"Who is this Maggie person you want to introduce me to?" Elizabeth interrupted her musings.

"She's another friend I've met while I've been here."

"And why is it so important that I meet her?"

"She's the same age as you for one thing, but she's also an artist. Something I know you're interested in. You'll like her."

Fortunately, Maggie was home when Grace knocked on her door and introduced her mother.

"Well I never. So this is your mother," Maggie said. "How do you do?" She offered her hand.

Elizabeth raised her eyebrows in surprise. "Charmed I'm sure."

"Come on in." Maggie stepped aside, so they could enter. "Sit yourself down while I put the kettle on."

"Please don't go to any trouble on my account," Elizabeth said.

"No trouble," she assured.

Grace helped Maggie with the preparations. Ten minutes later, the ladies enjoyed their tea and cake, among a cluster of trees, not far from the cabin.

"This cake is delicious. You must give me the recipe," Elizabeth said.

"I'm not the one you need to ask."

"I just assumed that you made it yourself," Elizabeth said.

"I'm not much of a cook, I'm afraid. I leave that to Albert."

"So Albert is your cook?"

Maggie laughed. "I guess you could call him that. But mostly, he's my husband."

"Your husband does the cooking?" Elizabeth said, as she regarded the concoction on her fork with new eyes.

"He sure does. My talents lie elsewhere."

"You remember, I told you that Maggie is an artist, Mother."

"Of course. I just thought that you'd still be responsible for taking care of the household chores as well. The only cooking Larry will do is around the barbecue!"

"Larry's your husband?" Maggie waited for confirmation. At a nod from Elizabeth, she continued. "I understand. You're from a traditional household, where men and women have their roles to play, and no one questions it?"

"What's wrong with that?" Elizabeth asked, defensively.

"There's nothing wrong with it, if that's what you both want." She waited a moment. "That is what you both want, isn't it?"

"Oh course. Why wouldn't I want it like that? It was good enough for my mother and her mother before that." Elizabeth's voice lost its strength.

Maggie leaned over to pat Elizabeth's hand. "I didn't mean to put you on the spot like that. It's just that I've always been a rather outspoken woman who knows what she wants. Albert knew when he married me that I wouldn't be spending all my time in the kitchen. And he was still willing to put up with me. Bless his heart."

"It is a rather unorthodox arrangement in this day and age," Elizabeth said.

"Things are changing," Maggie pointed out.

Elizabeth's pensive gaze turned toward the nearby trees that carried the earthy scent of pine on wafts of warm air.

"Are you all right Mother?" Grace asked.

"Oh, excuse me," she said absentmindedly.

"I don't blame you for enjoying the view," Maggie said, diverting attention away from Elizabeth's contemplation. "The landscape is inspiring. That's why I return here year after year — to capture it on canvas."

Elizabeth smiled and took her cue gratefully. "You must paint landscapes."

"Usually," she smiled. A silent understanding passed between them.

"Where did you study?"

"France and England when I could. But mostly, I stayed in Canada and studied with other Canadian artists. Being able to study painting in my own country had a huge impact on my work. The landscape here is wild and natural, just the way I like it.

"Do you have any of your work here?" Elizabeth asked, her eyes alight with interest.

"In the spare room if you'd like to see."

"I'd be delighted," Elizabeth said.

Paintings of all kinds were scattered about the spare bedroom. Some were stacked against the walls, while others were hung. One painting rested on an easel by the window, presumably to dry. There was an old beat up table beside the easel, covered in paint splotches, where she kept her pallet, paints, rags, and a can of mineral spirits for diluting paint and doing clean-ups.

Elizabeth studied the vibrant colors of Maggie's work. Up close her paintings looked like a kaleidoscope of color. But when you stepped back and took in the whole, everything came into focus. "You're very talented," she said.

"I can't take all the credit," Maggie said. "My inspiration comes from other Canadian artists — particularly the Group of Seven. They wanted to create a distinct Canadian identity through their work. The 1900s was an exciting time to be painting. So much was going on: Expressionism, Cubism, and Fauvism. European paintings of the time tended to be rather tame. That image doesn't fit Canada at all. It's much bigger — more rugged. The work of Group of Seven reflects that."

"I agree," Elizabeth said. "You were blessed to be a part of it."

"I was that," Maggie agreed.

"Did you ever get to meet any of the greats?"

"Here and there."

"How exciting. You must tell me all about it sometime."

The three women continued to study the rest of the paintings, while they talked about Maggie's experiences in art world of Montreal and British Columbia. She had even been to New York to see the Armory Show in 1913. Time just flew by, as they talked. Before they knew it, it was time to leave.

Grace put her arm through Elizabeth's, as they walked along the rocky path. "I had no idea you knew so much about art."

"You're not the only one whose interests lie beyond the kitchen," Elizabeth replied.

Grace contemplated her mother's remark the rest of the way back to camp.

XIX

"I'm sorry I have to leave you like this Mother, but I'm scheduled to work today."

"Don't worry about me dear, I'll just sit here and catch up on some reading," Elizabeth replied.

"I should be home by six — earlier if I can manage it."

"All right darling. Have a nice day."

One more day, Grace told herself, as she motored to work. She hadn't realized how much she had come to enjoy her own company. Having her mother constantly under foot was trying at best. Although, she had to admit, she was a little surprised at how well she got along with Maggie. Maggie was so bohemian, while her mother was, well, her mother. Grace walked into the diner to the clatter of dishes coming from the kitchen.

"How are things going with your ma?" Mary asked as soon as Grace walked through the swinging door to the kitchen.

"Not bad." Grace gathered the silverware to set the tables. "But I'll be glad when I can have the place to myself again."

"She is a strong presence, isn't she?"

"You could say that," Grace chuckled.

"It's hard to believe that she's your mother. You're so different."

"My mother's always telling me that I take after my father."

"Is that good?" Mary grabbed a towel to remove a pan of muffins from the oven. The aroma of rhubarb and burnt sugar filled the air.

"I think so. My father wasn't around very much while I was growing up, but when he was, we had fun. I get my love of the outdoors from him — and books. We both love to read."

Their conversation subsided while Grace prepared the tables in the dining room. She made sure there were plenty of napkins in the silver dispensers, and the salt and pepper pots were full.

"What did he do for a living?" Mary asked when Grace returned to the kitchen to prepare the batter for the pancakes.

"He worked in insurance. I remember he was gone a lot. You know how it is — people are only free in the evenings and such." She shrugged.

"That kind of shines a new light on things."

"What do you mean?" Grace paused in the middle of adding an egg to the flour and milk already in the bowl.

"Sounds like your mother had to manage on her own a lot. Might explain why she's a might over-bearing."

"I never thought of that, but you're probably right." She whipped up the batter and set it aside.

"I guess that gives you two something in common, after all."

"What?"

"Your mother already knows what it's like to be alone."

"Hmmm," Grace replied, deep in thought.

Grace had no further opportunity to think about her mother. She was rushed off her feet most of the morning. Things let up for a while around 11:15 am. The lull allowed Grace the time to wash and stack dishes, clean off tables, and make sure that a fresh pot of coffee was ready for the lunch crowd.

Maggie and Albert joined the lunch hour crunch.

"What can I get you today?" Grace asked, order pad in hand.

"Just coffee and some of Mary's apple pie for me," Maggie said.

"Make that two," Albert chorused.

"Are you sure you don't want anything else? Our special today is pork chops."

"Just pie and coffee thanks," Maggie said.

Grace cut two slices of the apple pie, poured the coffee, and returned to their table.

"I must say, I really enjoyed meeting your mother," Maggie said.

"Thanks. She enjoyed it too."

"She's certainly knowledgeable about art, isn't she?"

"She is. That surprised me. I knew she was interested in art, but I had no idea how much she already knew."

"She's not at all as I imagined."

"She's becoming a bit of a surprise to me as well."

"What do you mean?"

"She seems more – approachable lately -- not about everything, but about some things," she qualified. "Well, I must get back to work," Grace said.

By the time Grace got home that night, the only thing she had on her mind was enjoying a cup of tea and soaking her feet in a bowl of hot soapy water. The last thing she expected to find, when she walked through the door, was her mother in tears. Grace hurried to her side to offer comfort. "Mother are you all right?

Elizabeth pushed Grace away. "It's nothing dear."

"Something must have made you cry."

"I'm crying," she sputtered, "because I'm starting to understand."

"What do you mean?"

"All those years of trying to do the right thing — to be the right kind of woman..."

"And what kind of woman is that?"

"So bloody self-sacrificing," Elizabeth said with self-deprecation.

"Where did this come from?"

"I've been thinking about Maggie and the kind of relationship she has with her husband. I never dreamed it could be like that."

"You mean the fact that Albert takes care of all the cooking and baking?" Grace asked.

"And the fact that she has the freedom to paint whenever she wants."

Grace chuckled.

"Are you laughing at me?" Elizabeth demanded, eyes smudged with mascara and tears.

Grace reached out and hugged her mother amid a cloud of Chanel perfume. "Not at you exactly. It's just that I'm so relieved to know you finally understand why I want to work."

"I'm beginning to see how much the world has changed from when I was a young bride. Since your father retired, he's been trying to tell me how to run the house. Maybe I should let him. It's just that, I've managed very nicely on my own for years, without his help, thank you very much."

"Is that why you're here Mother? To get away from Daddy?"

Elizabeth started to cry again. She pulled a handkerchief from her sleeve to dry the tears and blow her nose. "I feel so ashamed."

"Don't be ashamed for being honest about your feelings."

"You know yourself, your father was hardly ever home," she hiccupped.

"I know. That must have been hard for you."

"It was. I was so lonely. I know I had you, but..." She looked into her daughter's eyes. "I'm sorry to say this, but it wasn't enough."

"Of course it wasn't. Just the same way my boys weren't enough for me. I always felt like I was missing something. I think maybe that's one of the reasons I agreed to participate in the sweat ceremony. I was tired of not being able to do the things I wanted to.

"But it's so different..."

"That's the point, isn't it? Things change. I've changed. All my life I've tried to please others. Now I have the chance to please myself."

"That's a pretty big responsibility," Elizabeth said.

"You should know. All those years Daddy was away, you took care of everything."

Elizabeth shrugged it off with the wave of a hand. "Oh that was nothing."

"Pardon me, but it seems like it was a very big thing."

Elizabeth wrung her hands together. "I don't suppose your father thinks it's a big thing. In fact, I don't think he even realizes that I am a capable woman at all."

"Maybe you need to educate him," Grace smiled.

Elizabeth squeezed her daughter's hand and laughed. "Maybe I should at that."

"Feel better now?" Grace asked.

"Much better. Thank you darling," Elizabeth said, her eyes still shimmering with tears. "I think I understand you a little better now."

"Do you Mother? Do you really?"

Elizabeth looked at her daughter with a glint in her eyes. "I think perhaps I might. I'm so proud of you dear, for having the courage to change your life."

"Oh my," Grace said, hand to her chest, "I think I'm going to cry."

"It's true. I've been so busy holding on to the past that I couldn't see it."

"I don't know about you, but I could use a drink. Why don't I open a bottle of wine while we cook dinner?"

Elizabeth reached up to caress her daughter's cheek. "That sounds lovely."

Grace's heart felt full, as they worked quietly side by side. Grace cooked the bacon for club sandwiches, while Elizabeth toasted bread and sliced tomatoes.

"I think that perhaps if I had something else to occupy my time and talents, I wouldn't have been so upset with your father for trying to run things at home," Elizabeth said when they sat down to eat.

"That's quite possible," Grace answered. "So, what are you going to do about it?"

"I don't know. I'm too old to go to work."

"But isn't there something you've always wanted to do?"

"Well, the happiest time in my life was when you were little."

Grace leaned across the table to take her mother's hand. "That's a lovely thing to say."

"It's true," Elizabeth answered, her emotions still close to the surface.

"If that's true, why is it that you and Daddy never had any more children?"

"I never told you this before, but I had a hard time of it when I was pregnant with you. The doctor said I wasn't to have any more children."

"I had no idea."

"How could you? You were a baby yourself. Maybe that's why I've always been so protective of you."

"That explains a lot. I wish you could have told me before."

"Would it have made a difference?"

"I don't know, but at least I would have understood."

"Perhaps so, but that doesn't help me solve my current problem. What am I going to do about your father?"

"Maybe it's not Daddy that needs to change."

Elizabeth's eyes popped open in surprise. "What are you suggesting?"

"Maybe this is your opportunity to do something you want. Isn't there some kind of work you can do with children, if that's what you want?"

"Like what?"

"I don't know. Maybe you could help out in a school or library."

"I'm not qualified to work in either environment."

"You don't need a degree to teach children to read. Or you could do story time at the library."

"Your father might not like the idea of my taking on such a project."

Grace smiled conspiratorially. "That's true, he might not."

Elizabeth was shocked. "Are you suggesting that I should do it anyway?"

Grace nodded. "I wish I had gotten a job when I wanted to despite Charles's misgivings. Perhaps I'd be better able to take care of myself now that he's gone."

"But I can't just leave your father alone."

"Why not? You're no good to him if you continue to spend your time together unhappy."

"I suppose that's true."

"Maybe if you got out of the house more, he might do the same."

"Maybe once I get him out of the house, I could move back in." They both laughed.

Dear Charles: July 11, 1963

I've barely had a minute to myself since my mother surprised me with a visit this week. She's going home tomorrow, so I can look forward to quiet evenings once again. Don't get me wrong, it hasn't been all bad. In fact her visit turned out rather nice.

When I got home from work tonight she was crying. As you know, she was never one to display emotion, so it felt strange to be the one doing the comforting. It was nice to see this side of her. I do believe we became more than just mother and daughter in that moment.

I never realized this before, but it was hard for her when Daddy worked all the time. I never really thought of her as an independent woman. But she was the one who took care of everything while Daddy was away. So she knows something of what it's like to live alone. Now that Daddy's retired, he's driving her crazy taking over everything. I think that's the reason she decided to visit me. It had nothing to do with checking up on me like I first thought. She even said I was courageous for trying to change my life. Mary's tried to tell me the same thing, but I wouldn't listen. If someone else had told me they'd left all that was familiar to visit another part of the country, I'd think they were brave. Why can't I look at myself in the same way? Yes, it was a very good visit. Not only that, but I think we've established a new direction for our relationship. And I find I'm rather glad about that.

Your wife,

Grace.

XX

The next day Elizabeth got ready to return to Toronto and her husband. Mother and daughter departed with hugs and a promise from Elizabeth to come back for another visit before the end of summer. Grace felt surprisingly lonely, and a might restless, after her mother left. Then an idea took root in her mind and wouldn't let go. She wanted to take an overnight canoe trip. Naturally it wasn't something she could do alone. And there was only one person who could help her.

Grace thought nothing of the hush that came over the clientele, when she walked into the diner on Monday morning and helped herself to a cup of coffee.

"What's up kid?" Mary asked when Grace appeared in the kitchen.

"I was hoping to talk to you about something."

"Sure. What's on your mind?"

"I've been thinking about taking an overnight canoe trip," Grace said.

"Does this have anything to do with those diaries you've been reading?"

"It has certainly got me wondering what it would be like to camp out along the river."

Mary paused in the act of flipping a burger. "Oh boy. You don't want much do you?"

"What, you think I can't do it?"

"Not alone, that's for sure." Mary placed slices of cheese on each sizzling burger, pressed the spatula on top, and lifted them onto the toasted buns. "Order up."

"Look, I know I've never done anything like this before. But everyone has to start somewhere."

"Mmmm," Mary considered, as she cleaned off the grill with her spatula and started work on her next order.

"I was hoping the boys could take me," Grace said hopefully. "They've lived on the river all their lives."

"That they have. But you haven't. It could be dangerous."

"I know, but lots of people do it, so how bad could it be?"

"It's one thing to take up residence in a cottage for the summer, but it's quite another matter to rough it in the wilds for a few days."

"You're not making this very easy for me," Grace pointed out.

"I just want to make sure you know what you're getting yourself into." Mary stood with one hand on her hip while still holding the spatula in the other. "It will mean spending your days paddling dangerous waters, your hands covered in blisters, and your back aching until you think you're gonna scream. Then there's the nights of camping out in rough terrain worrying about rattlesnakes and bad weather."

"I've been canoeing before, so I'm not exactly a novice."

"That's nothing compared to this. You'll have to worry about rough water. You could end up capsizing. And you'll be expected to portage. That means carrying a canoe and supplies over land. That's hard work. Do you think you can handle all that?" Mary turned her attention back to the grill.

At Mary's words, Grace began to question her own ability. What if everything Mary said was true? Maybe she was getting in over her head.

Mary sighed and touched Grace on the arm. "Why don't you at least sleep on this for tonight, and we'll talk again tomorrow." When Grace didn't reply, Mary offered, "I'm not saying no, I just think you need to be sure that you want to do this."

Grace gazed at her friend, nodded, and quietly turned to leave. She expected to have to defend her choices with her mother, but she never expected she'd have to convince Mary to help her. She decided to take a walk. She headed down the road and soon found herself at the entrance of a path she knew lead to Recollet Falls. She hadn't been there yet. Now was as good a time as any.

Dry pine needles covered the rocky trail through the woods. And tree roots intertwined, on the rocky surface, creating a natural ladder for climbing over the many hills along the path. It was dark in places, and at times it seemed like she was walking away from the river, but still she continued onward. The mosquitoes were the worst. She wasn't prepared for them. Her only line of defense was to wave her arms about erratically, so they wouldn't bite. But the action caused her to lose her balance, and she fell. "Oh!"

Thankfully, no bones were broken. She was more surprised than anything. When she got up to wipe the dirt off her shorts, she realized that she'd scraped her leg. Since it wasn't bleeding much, she continued on.

She could hear the river up ahead now — could see an open space in the trees. But first she had to get down a steep incline. She'd already fallen once and didn't want to chance it again. She might not be so lucky next time. She grabbed a nearby tree branch, made her way down in two big steps, and landed in a mud puddle. She wiped her feet off as best she could, followed the roar of the falls to its source, and found a spot to sit.

She was fascinated with how the water rushed over rocks and reached up like hands from the grave – deadly, if you didn't know what you were doing. It reminded Grace of Mary's words about the dangers of the river. Could Mary be right? Was she being foolish to even consider such an expedition?

She watched the water cascade over the falls, stretch out onto the horizon, and curve out of sight. Voyageurs and friars alike had travelled this route at one time or another. In fact, according to George, a group of Recollet Friars died at this very spot in the 1600s. And many more no doubt. If seasoned voyageurs could die in these waters, what chance did she have?

She made her way back to the path with a heavy heart. Once again it was necessary to pay attention to where she was going. But her confidence soon increased, as she moved deeper into the woods. The mosquitos were mercifully kind to her on the return trip, and she soon made her way back to the main road.

Mary was waiting for her at the dock. "Where the hell have you been?"

"I went for a walk to Recollet Falls. I understand now why you don't want me to go on this trip," Grace said.

"It's not that I don't want you to go, I just want you to be sure you know what you're getting yourself into."

Grace nodded. "After that little walk, I understand more than you know."

"Good," Mary nodded. "Then it's settled."

"Not exactly."

"What do you mean?"

"I said I understand the dangers better now, but I still plan to go."

"You're not making any sense."

"I'm tired of being afraid. I want to be like the voyageurs and live life on my own terms. Despite the dangers, I have to do this."

"Well hell!" Mary said. "I guess that's that."

"Does that mean you'll help me?" Grace smiled.

"I must be out of my mind, but I suppose it does," Mary said, shaking her head.

Grace was ecstatic until she realized that if anything went wrong, it would be all her fault. In order to calm her troubled thoughts, she wrote about them as soon as she got home.

Dear Charles: July 17, 1963

What have I done? I've convinced Mary and the boys to take me on an overnight canoe trip. We're to leave on Friday. That's only two days away. There's so much to do to get ready. The question is, am I ready? I've never done anything like this before. I know, I know. I need to get over my fears. And I want to. It's just, do I have to put myself in danger to do it? Not only that, I might be putting my friends in danger as well. What if something bad happens? I know it can. If it does, I guess it will mean I'll be seeing you sooner than I planned. Yet people do this kind of thing all the time and come back to tell the tale. James and Will know what they're doing -- so does Mary for that matter. Everything will be all right. I need to trust, or as Mr. Whitefeather says, "Have faith." And what was it you said to me that day? Oh yes, "Believe." Is this what you were talking about? That I need to believe in myself. Well, I guess there's only one way to get over my fear and that is to forge my way through it. OK, I think I'll be all right now. I'll just take it one step at a time. The first order of business is to start packing and keep telling myself, "All will be well."

Love,
Grace.

Grace kept herself busy over the next couple of days. Fortunately she had shifts at the diner to keep her thoughts occupied. It was only during the nighttime hours that her thoughts drifted toward the possible dangers of this journey. Somehow she would get through it. She had to if she wanted to live with herself.

XXI

The morning they set off on their trip, there was a light mist coming off the river. All was quiet, except for the eerie sound of a loon's haunting cry in the distance, and the gentle swish of the paddle, as it slid through the water. The quartet dressed in layers in deference to the cool morning. Grace knew it wouldn't last. The sun would soon burn through the mist, and they would be forced to toss their extra clothing aside to accommodate the changing mood of Mother Nature.

Fortunately, visibility improved by the time they encountered their first rapid. It was blessedly brief. Grace was too scared to be exhilarated, as the boys were wont to be. They hollered and shouted with glee, as they whipped across the tumbling waves. Even Mary was laughing. By the time they encountered their second rapid, Grace had a better idea of what to expect. This one was longer, but they were prepared. James sat at the back of the canoe and shouted out directions. Grace was on tenterhooks, when it became time to maneuver their craft through this second hurdle, but she said nothing. She was the one who wanted to go on this trip after all. She wasn't about to let them down.

As promised, Grace's back hurt, and she was developing blisters on her hands. Despite this, she enjoyed the constant pull of the paddle sliding through the water.

By mid-morning, Mary called a halt from the second canoe. She was hot and wanted to discard a few layers of clothing. Everyone followed her lead. They also took the time to have a snack, of dried fruit and nuts with water, to keep up their energy.

They were on their way much too soon. Grace wondered how on earth the voyageurs managed to keep up this kind of pace. Their canoes were so much bigger and heavier, as well as being packed with furs, people and provisions. They could weigh up to 3 tons, if she recalled correctly. If ever she wanted to have a sense of what those men had to deal with every day, this was it. The constant pattern of paddling and switching sides was hypnotic. The only thing that kept her going was the knowledge that she was living her dream.

"Rapids," James yelled when they approached another surge of water up ahead.

Their only hope was to try to keep the canoe steady and ride it out. She had to admit, at times it was rather exhilarating flying across the waves, as though the front of the canoe prepared for lift off. But mostly, Grace was scared to death of tipping over. Just when she was beginning to wonder if they'd ever get to the end of the torrent, the boat began to slow down, along with the beating of her heart.

Grace was relieved when James finally called a halt to stop for lunch.

As they rowed toward an outcrop of land, they startled a lone heron in the shallows. Grace was captivated. Her eyes followed its path above their heads. It was so close she could feel the air pull and shift beneath its wings, while droplets of water spattered across her arms and face. From a distance, it reminded her of a Pterodactyl.

When the bottom of the canoe scraped against stone, James and Will jumped into the shallow water and pulled their respective canoes toward the small island. Grace and Mary were soon into the fray, squealing as their hot bodies hit the prehistoric water. They hauled the canoes onto dry land, so the hull would no longer scrape against the stony surface of the French River System.

James proposed they take it easy for the remainder of the day. No one objected —least of all Grace. Mary decided to gather wood for their fire. The boys found a rock, from which they could dive into the water. Grace, on the other hand, found a nice shady spot to take a nap, and though she was certainly tired enough, she hurt too much to sleep.

They decided to eat an early supper when the sun took cover behind some clouds, and the wind began to pick up. They were just clearing away the dishes, when lightening shot across the sky, followed closely by the rumble of thunder. They rushed around to stash everything beneath their overturned canoes, so they could keep it dry. The small group didn't fare as well, however. The shelter, which had protected Grace from the burning sun that afternoon, did little to prevent the wind-driven deluge from penetrating their niche inside the tent. The ground was wet, and the air was cold, so they huddled together in their rain gear and waited for nature's fury to unfold. They were miserable. The rain continued on late into the night. When it finally did stop, there was no point in moving, for there wasn't a dry spot to be had anywhere.

The next morning couldn't come soon enough for the tired troop. They moved their stiff bodies about without a word. There was no dry wood to start a fire, so they ate a cold meal of fruit and nuts. After breakfast, they scouted around the island to see what effects the storm had wrought. Apart from an abundance of water, and the occasional downed tree branch, the damage was surprisingly minimal. They spied a purple finch taking a bath in a puddle. Myrtle warblers and song sparrows cried out from the dampened tree branches. And they startled a rabbit into flight beneath a nearby fir tree. It was as though the wildlife were celebrating the brand new day — probably because they had slept better than the ragged troop.

"We'd better head out now," Will said.

Despite their tiredness, and the lack of a decent breakfast, it was necessary to be alert in order to steer their way through the rolling waters. It took all of Grace's resources to focus on the work ahead.

"We'll be coming up to a rapid soon," James called out, when their craft began to pick up speed.

"Don't you think we should portage here?" Mary yelled over the distant roar of the impending rapids.

"We can make it," James assured her. "I've been through a lot worse than this."

Mary chanced a glance toward Will, but he was busy trying to keep their own canoe under control, as it bounced around wildly.

"Hang on," James bellowed. There was no turning back now. The force of the water propelled them headlong into the swell. The canoe bucked and bobbed, as it accelerated. "Hard to starboard," he yelled over the crashing waves. "That's it, keep it steady."

Water splashed over the side of the canoe and drenched them, as they surged across the swell and came perilously close to a craggy outcrop. Just when they thought they'd be safe, the back of the canoe collided with a concealed rock that sent James head-first into the maelstrom.

Someone screamed.

James was swept along the raging waters. His head disappeared every few seconds, as he fought the galloping waves.

"Hold on," Grace yelled. Somehow, she had to save him from being smashed against the rocks. Mary barked orders at Will, while their own craft careened precariously over the waves.

Grace struggled to get their canoe as close to James as she could without actually colliding into him. "Grab on." As the seconds ticked by, James made a lunge for the boat. But Grace couldn't keep it steady. He disappeared from sight.

"Oh God. Please. No," Grace screamed over the thundering rapids. To her relief, his head soon appeared once again. He sputtered and cursed, but he was all right. Thank God he was a strong swimmer.

Grace was exhausted. But there was no alternative but to try again. With every stroke of the paddle, her arms trembled, but she pushed herself forward. Then, it was as though a hand reached down to place everything into perfect alignment. The river lifted James up, the canoe did a nosedive, and somewhere in the middle the two converged. Grace braced herself for the impact. The canoe tilted to the side, and they took on more water, but James didn't let go, until Grace got them to safety.

James hauled himself over the side and collapsed into the bottom of the boat. "What a wild ride!" he howled, right before he leaned over the side of the canoe and retched.

"He's swallowed a lot of water," Mary shouted. "We'd better get off the river."

Once they found an accessible landing spot, Grace struggled to heave the canoe to shore. Mary and Will came over to haul James onto solid ground.

Grace stumbled breathlessly toward them. "Will he be all right?"

"I think so," Mary answered. "He just needs to rest."

Because of their forced exit off the river, the campsite they chose was not the most ideal. The dense vegetation, coupled with the overnight rain, was a breeding ground for mosquitos.

"We can't stay here, Ma. The mosquitoes will eat us alive," James pointed out.

"Don't you think I know that?" Mary slapped yet another of the offending pests off her arm. "I just think we should rest a little before we push on."

"We're not gonna get any rest with all these mosquitoes around. You don't need to worry about me, Ma, I'm fine now," James assured her.

"You scared the shit outta me. If it hadn't been for Grace's quick thinking, I don't know what would have happened."

"Nothing's going to happen to me."

"That's the trouble with you young people, you think you're indestructible. I've only just lost your father, I don't want to lose you too."

"I'm sorry, Ma. I wasn't thinking. But I'm strong. I know this river."

"If you know the river so well, why did you fall overboard?"

"Stuff happens."

"Is that all you have to say for yourself?"

"Listen, Ma, I planned this trip the best I could, but you know?" He shrugged.

"And that's supposed to help?"

"I'm a good swimmer. I wasn't in any real danger."

"You may not have been in danger out there, but you're in plenty of trouble with me, buster. If you were small, I'd tan your hide for scaring me like that."

"Well, it's over now," James said softly.

Mary snorted.

"You know we can't stay here," James insisted.

Mary pressed her lips together and nodded.

Fortunately, it didn't take long to find a better spot high above the river. There was a nice wide open space, surrounded by deciduous trees, where a family of chipmunks had taken up housekeeping. The trees created a natural screen from prying eyes, if they wanted to use it as a latrine. And they were able to find some dry wood hidden beneath a thick layer of branches. They built a fire and eagerly looked forward to sharing a hot meal.

Once the camp was set up, the boys went fishing. Fortunately, their food supplies had been wrapped in oilskin, which kept it dry, during their wild ride.

"Are you all right?" Grace asked when she was alone with Mary.

"I will be. He gave me quite a scare," Mary said.

"I know, and I can't help but feel partly responsible. If it wasn't for me, we wouldn't be here."

"Grace."

"Hmmm?"

"Shut up!"

"I only meant..."

"Like my son pointed out to me, you can't plan for the unexpected. My boys love this river. Nothing, and no one, will ever keep them off it. Not you -- and certainly not me."

The boys came back to camp with some Pickerel for the frying pan. They ate the fish, with fried potatoes and greens, followed by sliced apples baked on the fire with sugar and cinnamon. They washed it all down with some strong black coffee. It went a long way to lift their spirits after a trying day.

Curious about her surroundings, Grace pulled herself stiffly to a standing position. "I'm going to explore for a while."

"Keep an eye out for rattlesnakes," Will called after her.

Grace blanched. "I thought your mother was only joking about the snakes."

"He's just trying to scare you," Mary assured her. "There are rattlesnakes in this area, but I've rarely ever come across one. If you leave them alone, they'll leave you alone."

Grace didn't know if Mary was telling the truth or just trying to reassure her. She settled on the latter. It wasn't long before she found a place to sit by the river. The muffled sounds of the camp faded into the background. The sky was clear, indeed, there wasn't a rain cloud in sight, thank goodness. They may actually get some sleep tonight. She was monetarily distracted by the antics of an otter playing in the water.

Grace felt strangely sad that their trip was almost over. Even though they'd been rained on, James had fallen into the river, and they'd nearly been eaten alive by mosquitoes, she felt a deep sense of satisfaction for accomplishing what she set out to do. She certainly felt physically stronger, but she felt mentally stronger as well. It was a good feeling.

"What are you thinking about?" Mary wanted to know, when she came to sit beside her friend.

"Oh, I was just thinking about how life is always changing."

"That's the way it goes, I guess."

"I know. It's those in-between times that are hard — when you're left treading water with no land in sight."

"I guess it's what we do with those in-between times that count," Mary philosophized.

* * * * * *

After a restful night, the party enjoyed a leisurely breakfast. It was a little breezy on the river, for the final leg of their journey, but nothing they couldn't handle. By mid-day, the sun shone brightly as though rewarding their efforts. Will started to sing, and one by one, the others joined in. Much like the voyageurs of old, singing helped to lift their spirits, as they neared their final destination.

"There's Hartley Bay," Will said. "It won't be long now before we're back at home."

XXII

Jack Malone, a friend of Mary's, piled their stuff into his rusty old pick-up truck for the trip home. While Grace and Mary squeezed into the cab with Jack, the boys were wedged in the back between the two canoes to prevent being bandied about every time they hit a bump in the road.

When they arrived home, Jack helped Mary and Will to unload their supplies and store their canoes in a shed at the back of Mary's place. Meanwhile, James transferred Grace's stuff to the family boat and escorted her back to Crow's Nest.

"What's wrong?" James asked, when Grace paused at her front door after they'd unloaded her stuff.

"My door's open. I'm sure I locked it before I left." She cautiously pushed the door all the way open and stepped into the room. "Oh my!"

"You wait here while I look around," James commanded when he got a look at the place. She'd been ransacked.

Despite James' directive, Grace followed cautiously behind him. She was shocked to see books and cushions littering the living room floor. She stepped over the debris to check out the bedroom. Dresser drawers were empty, and her things were strewn about the room. She noticed her journal was missing from its usual place on her bedside table. Indignant, she fumbled through the bedding and clothing, scattered around the room, to see if she could find it. It was one thing to destroy the material things of her life, but it was quite another to have a stranger get their hands on the letters she had written to her husband. It felt like a violation of their relationship, not to mention it exposed her most personal thoughts. Then a flash of red caught her eye, and she knew she'd found it. Whoever tossed it aside thought it was of no consequence. She brought it over to the bed, where she sat down and breathed a silent prayer of thanks. That's where James found her.

"It's the same everywhere," he said.

Grace looked up. "Who would do such a thing?"

James shook his head. "I don't know, but you can't stay here tonight. You'd better come home with me."

She nodded and rose from the bed with the journal still clutched in her hand. The kitchen hadn't fared any better. Broken dishes were in a heap on the floor. From the scratch marks and chips on the wall, it looked as though someone had thrown them against the wall first. She shook her head. "I just don't understand."

James took Grace by the arm and led her away from the destruction. "Come on, let's get you home."

Grace was numb.

"What happened?" Mary said, surprised to see Grace in such a state of shock.

"Someone has ransacked Grace's place," James explained.

Mary took right over. "James, you call the police. I'll take care of Grace."

"I don't understand. I didn't bring anything of value with me," Grace explained to the police officer sometime later. "I only brought a few clothes and some food."

The officer explained that it wasn't unheard of for people to experience a break and enter, especially during the summer, when more people come to the area.

"So you're saying there's no way of knowing who committed this crime?" Grace asked.

"It was likely some young kids out for a lark," the officer said. "But whoever did this is probably long gone by now."

Grace didn't know whether to be comforted by that or not.

"We'll have one of our officer's check around the place for any signs of further trouble. Other than that, I suggest that if you do find anything missing, let us know."

"Thank you officer," Mary said and led him to the door.

"Do you really think the officer was right -- that this was just a fluke and there's nothing to worry about?" Grace asked.

"It does seem like the most likely explanation," Mary answered.

Despite what the officer said, Grace couldn't help but worry about the vandalism of her home. As she lay in bed that night, she found it hard to imagine why anyone would want to do such damage just for the fun of it. It was particularly disheartening after their trek along the river. It was too much.

Dear Charles: July 21, 1963

Where do I begin? So much has happened during the past few days. Some of it good, and some -- not so much. Do you want the bad news or the good news first? Maybe if I start with the bad news, we can end on a high note.

My cabin was ransacked while I was away on my overnight canoe trip. -- Can you believe it? I actually went on a canoe trip. — But more on that later. Someone broke into my cabin and just flung everything all over the place. God knows why. The police seem to think it's an isolated incident, like that's supposed to make me feel better. I know that most of the things weren't mine, but still. My biggest worry was the loss of my journal, as you can imagine, but I guess whoever did all that damage wasn't interested in a woman's ramblings. To think that someone might have damaged the only connection I still have with you is unimaginable. Not that I could ever forget you, but I take such comfort in our regular dialogue. I'll have to hide it in the future. Not that this will ever happen again, so please don't worry about me. I've made some good friends here at the French River. They look out for me.

Now for the good news. I survived the canoe trip. Mary was reluctant at first. She thought I was getting in over my head. And maybe I was. People don't seem to think I'm very capable. What does that say about me? Was I always such a lightweight? But I'm glad I did it just the same. It was something I felt I had to do. It seems that since you've been gone, I've had to struggle to do a lot of things without you.

I must remember to be kind with myself. I'm a beginner at so many things. I took for granted you'd always be there. I guess that was my mistake. It hasn't always been easy, but I've tried to muddle through. Some things I've done better than others. Like I actually helped to save James' life when he fell overboard. Can you imagine? I don't know I did it. I just acted on instinct. If anything happened to James it would be like it happened to one of our own boys. It's true, these people have become like family to me. I guess when you go through a trip such as ours, it has a tendency to bring you closer. I couldn't be more thrilled about it. I don't know how they feel about me, but I do know they have been there for me from the beginning. It's been a long day, and I'm tired. Until next time.

Good night my love,
Grace.

* * * * * *

Grace felt strange walking into her cabin after what happened the night before. It didn't feel like hers anymore. She knew that was ridiculous, because lots of people have spent the summer in this rental property. Still, she couldn't shake the feeling that whoever broke in had left their imprint on everything.

James began by shovelling the broken dishes into the garbage, so no-one would get hurt. Grace decided that since the shelves were already bare, it was a good time to give them a thorough cleaning. It also helped to wash away the presence of her unknown and most unwelcome guest. She replaced the broken dishes with donated ones from the diner. She worked on the book case next. By the time she made it into the bedroom, she realized nothing had been stolen. Perhaps the officer was right and some summer visitor had been out to cause mischief.

George turned up later that afternoon. "Mary told me what happened."

"It seems that it was just some isolated incident," Grace explained.

"It must have been quite a shock to come home and find your things strewn about."

"Technically, most of the things weren't mine. They belong to the owner. But yes, it was a bit of a shock," she replied, trying to downplay the incident.

"Well, I'm glad you're all right. Will you be O.K. by yourself tonight?"

"I'm sure I'll be fine," Grace answered with false bravado. "Whoever did this is probably long gone by now."

"You're right of course."

When Albert and Maggie showed up, they shared a knowing glance upon seeing her with George. "We heard you had a little trouble last night and came to help."

"Everyone is being so kind, but I think we have everything under control," she said.

George took a step back. "Well, I'd better get back. I just wanted to make sure you're O.K. If you need anything..."

Grace placed a reassuring hand on his arm. "Thank you George. It was nice of you to be so concerned."

"Does George come out here to see you often?" Maggie asked after George left.

"Of course not. That wouldn't be appropriate. How could you ask such a thing?"

"We just don't want you to get hurt, that's all."

"He's only offering support, much like you and Albert," she pointed out.

"Come on Mother, we'd better let Grace get on with her work," Albert urged his wife with a nudge.

"Thanks for the offer of help." Grace watched them disappear around the side of the cabin.

The boys left shortly after. Grace waved them off at the dock and wondered what to do with herself. The scent of pine sol filled the air, as she walked into the living room. She soon had a tray of crackers and cheese ready to take to the river. The rocking of the hammock, combined with a full tummy, made Grace sleepy. But just as her eyes started to close, she shook herself awake and looked cautiously around. She got up and went back inside. She locked the door and headed for the bedroom. She was asleep as soon as she lay down.

* * * * * *

Something wasn't right. She thought she heard a motor boat, but that could have been in her dreams. The sound seemed so far away. Then she heard an "Oomph!" followed by swearing outside. She struggled to see in the waning light, when the heavy tread of footsteps on the deck called her to action. She swung her tiny feet over the side of the bed and hurried to the window to look out. But she couldn't see from this angle. When someone pounded on the door, she started to sweat. Her eyes quickly darted around the room for some kind of weapon. Her hands alighted on the lamp beside the bed. She yanked the cord out of the socket, tossed the shade on the bed, and ran on tiptoe to the front door. "Who's there?"

"Open the door, it's just me." The voice was muffled through the wooden panel, but she recognized who it was.

With shaky fingers, Grace struggled with the lock, threw the door open, and found James standing on her doorstep. "What are you doing out here this time of night?" she admonished and stood back to allow him to enter before locking the door.

"It's only ten o'clock," he said. "Mom wanted me to find out if you'd like some company tonight."

"You scared me half to death," she said. She placed the lamp she was holding on a nearby table.

"Sorry. I thought you'd still be up."

"I must have been really tired, because I fell asleep shortly after you left."

James tossed his kit on the sofa. "Just tell me where you want me to sleep, then you can go back to bed."

"I'm much too wound up to sleep now. How about some hot chocolate?"

James helped himself to the cookies, while Grace warmed some milk in a saucepan on the stove. When it was ready, she poured and stirred the mixture and placed the saucepan in the sink to soak.

"Doing something as simple as enjoying a cup of cocoa makes everything feel almost normal again."

"I know what you mean. When Mom's got something on her mind, she likes to bake."

Grace nodded.

"Are you worried?" James asked.

Grace didn't need to ask what he meant. She knew he was referring to her intruder. "The thought has crossed my mind," Grace answered.

In James own inimitable way he said, "I wish I could promise that this will never happen again," he began. "But no one can promise that."

He had Grace's full attention now.

"At the same time, you can't sit around waiting for the worst to happen. If you do that, then they've won," he finished.

Grace wasn't accustomed to people speaking so frankly. She was used to a more soothing response that was designed to ease her worries. But he was right, she couldn't let this beat her. And there was comfort in that. She gathered their empty cups and put them in the sink to soak along with the saucepan. "Come on," she said. "I'll show you to your room.

* * * * * *

Grace was eating toast and peanut butter when James walked into the kitchen the following morning. "Can I get you anything?" she asked.

"Naa, coffee will do." He poured himself a cup of coffee with two sugars and milk; then he grabbed two pieces of toast, slathered them with peanut butter and strawberry jam, and took a big bite.

Grace couldn't help but smile.

"What?" he said, his mouth full of food.

"I thought you weren't hungry," she answered.

"I lied," he said, giving her a mischievous grin that made her laugh. Suddenly the events of the past two days slipped away.

"So, what are you up to today?" James asked.

"Oh look." Grace interrupted when she saw a bird fly past the window and land in front of the kitchen window. She picked up her binoculars to get a closer look. According to her book of birds, it was a yellow-shafted flicker. They watched it spatter dirt into the air, with its long-spiked bill, in its search of its next meal. Suddenly Grace knew exactly what she wanted to do with her day.

After James left to help his brother work in the family vegetable garden, Grace gathered her binoculars and sun hat and set out to do some bird watching.

She watched a blue heron, as it moved with careful grace along the river bank; she saw a robin feeding its young in an old pine tree; as well as a black and white warbler in the same tree; followed by a purple finch, but it flew by so fast, she couldn't quite make out its markings.

After a while, she decided to take a break. She leaned back on a flat rock, hands propped behind her for support, and felt its warmth seep through her palms. It was as though the vibration of the rock was infused into her very being. She was a part of the rock, and it was a part of her. Though the landscape shifted and changed, it was forever present. That, at least, was something she could count on. It was a comforting thought. Her mind drifted. She hadn't heard the mysterious singing in a long time. She missed it. It was like someone, or something, was watching over her.

"Am I disturbing you?" a voice asked.

Startled out of her reverie, Grace turned to find Albert standing behind her. "Don't mind me, I was just daydreaming," she smiled. "Are you looking for specimens?"

He held up the burlap bag he carried over one shoulder. "That I am. Mother was just talking about you this morning. How are you doing?"

"After roughing it for a few days, I'm feeling quite lazy today."

Albert chuckled. "Mother got a little worried when the weather turned bad."

"You and me both," Grace teased.

"Why don't you come over to the camp? Mother and I would enjoy hearing all about your adventure."

"Is she home at this time of the day?"

"She decided to stay home to put the finishing touches on one of her paintings."

Grace followed Albert the short distance to their camp.

"Mother. There's someone here to see you," Albert called out as he entered the front door.

"You don't have to yell. I may be old, but my hearing hasn't gone yet." When Maggie walked into the room and saw Grace, her face lit up. "I'm so glad you're here."

Grace was warmed by her reception and went over to hug her friend.

"Why don't you go and pot whatever you have in that bag, so Grace and I can get caught up?" Maggie said to Albert.

Albert smiled and nodded on his way out the door.

"Come, sit down and tell me about your trip," Maggie indicated the kitchen chair with the sweep of her arm. "We got worried when that big storm came up. How did you make out?"

"We got wet," Grace kibitzed.

"Don't get smart with me young lady. I'm old enough to be your mother."

"I'm sorry. The rain was a bit of a bother, but we managed. Those rapids after the storm; now that was the real challenge."

"You don't mean to tell me that James and Will took you through it instead of portaging?"

"They felt it would be fine. Besides, James and Will seemed to know what they were doing — until James got tossed overboard. Then I began to wonder."

"Oh, for land's sake! Someone could have drowned."

"As you can see, we didn't."

"Did you hear that Albert?" Maggie called out.

Albert came in from the porch, where he potted his plant. "I can hear fine, Old Woman, as you know very well." He washed his hands at the sink and joined them.

"So, what have I missed while I was away?" Grace asked when Albert pulled up a chair. "I've only been gone for a few days, but it feels like so much longer."

Albert and Maggie shared a look.

Grace looked back and forth between them. "What was that all about?

"You'd better tell her. It would be better coming from a friend, than if she heard from someone else." Albert poured himself some tea from the pot on the table.

"Tell me what?"

Maggie placed a hand over Grace's and took a deep breath. "There's a rumour in town that you've been seen keeping company with George Watson."

"You know it's true."

"There's more."

Grace waited.

"Someone saw you two kissing."

"Kissing?" Grace was aghast. "Well, whoever it was is quite mistaken."

"That may be so, except that you've also been seen leaving his home at night."

Grace jumped out of her chair and began to pace. "What are you implying?"

"I'm not implying anything. I...we, just thought you should know."

"I can't believe this is happening. This is why I left Toronto. What am I supposed to do; shut myself away?"

"Of course not. But people tend to misinterpret what they don't understand."

"Do you believe this rumour?"

"I believe that you would never do anything to intentionally hurt someone."

"It's true I spent an afternoon with George studying the Champlain diaries; and I did stay for dinner. But that was just because it was convenient. As for the kissing; it never happened."

Maggie paused to consider this information.

"Was there ever an incident that could have been misconstrued?" Albert interjected.

"Never," Grace said vehemently; then she blushed. "Oh dear." She sat back down. "There was this one time, but it was completely innocent," she explained. "It was the same night that Mr. Franco accused me of participating in the sweat ceremony. I told you about that."

"I remember," Maggie responded.

"Well, I was so upset when I got back to the camp, I decided to go for a long walk and got lost. By the time I managed to find my way back, it was getting dark, and there was a man waiting for me in front of the cabin. At first I thought it was Mr. Franco. I was so relieved when it turned out to be George. I started crying, and I just naturally turned to him for comfort. But that was all it was -- comfort. George loves his wife. He told me so. Besides, I'm not the kind of woman who would steal someone else's husband," Grace said, wringing her hands. "What should I do?"

Maggie and Albert stared at each other. "We can't decide that for you," Maggie said. "You have to look into your own heart, and do what you think is best."

"I can't just ignore him," Grace implored.

"You don't have to make a decision right now. But whatever you decide to do, we're behind you," Maggie assured her.

"Thank you," Grace said.

On her walk back to her cabin, Grace wondered when would be the best time to tell George that they had to end their friendship.

XXIII

When Grace arrived at work the next morning, conversation came to a halt when she entered the diner, and George Watson wasn't at his usual seat by the window. Just when she was starting to feel like she belonged, she now felt alienated because of a simple misunderstanding. It made her so mad.

"I'm so glad you're here. I need to talk to you," Mary said when Grace entered the kitchen.

"If it's about George, you needn't bother. Maggie already told me about the rumours."

"What are you gonna do?"

"The only thing I can do right now and that's get to work." Grace tied her apron and placed her order book and pencil into her pocket. She squared her shoulders and marched right out front.

By mid-afternoon, Grace's neck and shoulders hurt. It was such an effort to try to act as though everything was normal, when it was anything but. She knew people were gossiping about her. They stopped talking whenever she approached their table. When she had a break, she headed for the bathroom. It was there she broke down. George still hadn't come into the diner. She didn't know whether to be relieved or hurt. She threw cold water on her face to hide the telltale traces of her tears. She took a deep breath and went back to work.

Her heart skipped a beat when she saw Henry Franco sitting at one of her tables, and he wasn't alone. What was he doing here? But she supposed she knew the answer to that. Three other men sat with him whom she recognized as regulars. Funny, he didn't seem the type to have friends. She had no choice but to wait on him. She grabbed the coffee pot, along with four mugs, and took it to their table. With shaky hands, she poured the hot liquid into each container. "Are you ready to order?"

Everyone ordered the blueberry pie. But Franco wanted more time to decide. She came back a few minutes later with the requested pie.

"You know I think I will have a piece of that pie," Franco said.

Grace came back with his pie and placed it in front of him.

"How about some ice-cream on top of that." He slapped his fork against his palm as though impatient with the service.

On shaky legs, Grace walked back to get the ice cream and placed the dessert in front of him.

He scrutinized his fork and tossed it on the table. "Fork's dirty. I want another."

Grace was getting tired of this nonsense. She picked up the fork and thought about sticking him with it, but said, "There's nothing wrong with this fork."

"Are you calling me a liar? This fork is dirty. I want another."

Grace could hear the other men trying to calm him down over the buzzing in her ears. She couldn't allow this bully to get the better of her. She bit her lip. "Will that be all?"

Franco sized her up as though wondering how far he could push her. "You took long enough to get my pie. Now my coffee's cold."

"Is everything all right over here?"

To Grace's surprise, it was George who asked the question. "Everything's fine." She prayed he wouldn't interfere.

"Well, lookie here." Franco lifted his bulky frame from the table in an obvious effort to intimidate George. "I'm surprised you got the nerve to show your face around here, especially when everyone knows what you two have been up to."

George stood his ground. "Well, everyone is mistaken."

Franco glanced at his seat mates, to make sure he had their attention, before he replied. "You're a liar."

There was a deathly pause before one of Franco's comrades said, "Come on Henry, I think it's time we left." Franco ignored the man. He directed his next comment to Grace. "I'm a little tired of you city folk acting like you're better than everybody else. First you get chummy with them

Indians, now him." Franco prodded his powerful fingers into George's chest which made him stumble.

Grace stepped back, afraid he'd go for her next.

"Everyone knows what you two have been up to."

"That's enough." George spoke with controlled anger.

"A' course you'd deny it, but everyone knows the truth. What can you expect from a woman who gets involved in dirty Indian rituals? She's free and easy."

Grace's body shook with fury. "How dare you?" she hissed. Without thinking, Grace's open palm connected with Franco's cheek. Her hand flew to her hot face. She couldn't believe what she'd just done.

Franco reeled from the impact. His face was mottled with rage to the roots of his almost non-existent hair. His fists clenched and unclenched as he puffed himself up and bellowed. "How dare I? How dare you take part in God knows what kind of heathen nonsense. It's a blasphemy, that's what it is, a blasphemy."

"All right, I've heard enough out of you. I think it's time for you to leave." Mary stepped into the ruckus. Her able-bodied cook stood right behind her for support.

Franco folded his arms across his chest. "You can't make me do anything."

"I can when it disturbs my customers," Mary said, standing up to the much bigger man.

"Come on Henry, you've said enough. It's time to go." One of his buddies grabbed him by the arm, but Franco shrugged him off. The man raised his voice and tried again. "Franco, that's enough."

"You haven't heard the last of me," Franco yelled back, as his friends dragged him away. "You mark my words, folks around here don't cotton to such goings on."

"Are you all right?" Mary asked when the door closed behind Franco and his friends. "Come and sit down for a minute."

Grace's voice quivered. "I just want things to get back to normal." But when she looked around the diner, she knew that wasn't going to be possible. She was sure that by the end of the day, word would spread about this particular incident.

"What are you all staring at?" Mary blasted the remaining clientele. "Don't you have anything better to do than to listen to Henry Franco's lies?"

"Please Mary, let it be."

"I won't. Everyone knows what Henry's like. They've no business believing anything that man says."

"Please," Grace repeated.

"She's right," George interjected. "Perhaps it would be best if someone took Grace home."

"Nothing doing." Mary was adamant. "Grace, you're going to spend the night with me."

"I'll be fine."

"At least come into the kitchen, and sit down for a bit."

Grace didn't have the energy to argue.

"You'd better get on home. You're not helping matters by being here." Mary shooed George away with the wave of her arm.

"Wait," Grace interjected. "We need to talk," she said to George. She hoped Mary understood that she needed a few minutes alone with him.

"I'd better get back to cleaning the grill," Mary said.

The kitchen buzzed with activity, while Grace collected her thoughts.

"I know what you're going to say," George said. "I'm not an idiot. I know what people have been saying about us."

Grace met his gaze and said, "Yes. And there's only one thing to do to make them stop."

"Right," George responded in a monotone. "I guess this is goodbye."

"I'm afraid so." Grace already felt heavy with the loss of his friendship. She watched him walk away. The swinging door to the kitchen waved in his wake.

Mary was by her side in an instant. "You OK kid?"

Grace was finally able to collapse into a nearby chair.

"I'm sorry things had to end like this."

Grace experienced a deep sadness. "Franco only said what everyone else was thinking."

"People like to talk."

"Unfortunately, there is some truth to what Franco said."

"So what? Look, do you think I don't know that there are people around here who talk about me because I'm Ojibwe? But they're willing to turn a blind eye as long as I keep serving them coffee. I'm different and it scares them. You scare them."

"Oh Mary. I should have realized."

"What? That I'm Ojibwe, or that I scare people?"

"How can you joke about it?"

"Well I could cry and carry on about it if you'd like, but what good is that gonna do?"

"I see your point."

"Do you?"

"I think what you're trying to say is you can't change who you are."

"Damn right you can't. Not that I'd want to. I'm proud to be part of the Anishinaabe Nation. So why snivel about it? Look, just because you don't conform to the way people think you should act, it doesn't mean you should change anything."

"Me, non-conforming? I find that hard to believe. I've spent my whole life conforming."

"How many white people do you know would participate in an Ojibwe sweat ceremony?"

"Yes, but..."

"And now they see you spending time with a married man, and they don't like it."

"We did nothing inappropriate," Grace said defensively.

"And what about when you slapped old Franco across the face?"

Grace held her head in her hands. "I still can't believe I did that."

"Well, hell, he deserved it. He's nothing but a big bully preying on a woman like that. He thinks it makes him look like a big man. Phttt!"

"Look, my hands are still shaking."

Mary held Grace's hands close to her body and stared directly into her eyes for emphasis. "The point is, you don't fit the mold, so people are willing to believe whatever a blowhard like Franco tells them."

"I don't know what to say."

"There's nothing to say. That's just the way it is."

"I must get back to camp," Grace said after a while.

"Are you sure you don't want to stay for supper?"

"I don't think I could eat anything right now."

"If you're sure."

"I am. But thank you."

Grace blocked all thoughts from her mind beyond navigating her way home. She tied up the boat and slid her feet into the water. A light breeze shifted her hair into her eyes, and she brushed it away. She sighed and rubbed her temples, then she went inside to write in her journal.

Dear Charles: July 24, 1963

I've gone and done it this time. I became what I swore I wasn't — the other woman. Well, maybe that's a bit too harsh. Be that as it may, people seem to think I've been spending too much time with George Watson. The fact that his wife is out of town certainly doesn't help either. I knew it could happen, yet I chose to ignore my better judgement in order to spend time with him. It's not as though I wanted anything inappropriate from him. In all honesty, I do miss male companionship. But it's yours I'm wanting, not George's. I guess I just enjoyed my talks with him. They reminded me so much of our conversations. They were always lively and interesting.

Now Henry Franco's really stirred the pot by accusing us of wrong-doing. I still can't believe I slapped him, whether he deserved it or not. But I did it right in the middle of the diner for everyone to see. He's not going to forget that any time soon. Then I had to tell George that we can't be friends any more. But he already knew that. It's sad really, but I suppose that's the way it has to be.

Given my current circumstances, I don't know how Mary can say I don't conform to people's expectations. I am giving up my friendship with George, after all. It doesn't make sense. I've always been the good daughter, the good wife. Did something happen when I wasn't looking?

Grace.

XXIV

"George's wife came home last night," Mary said to Grace when she went in to work next day.

Grace's heart gave a little jolt. She wondered if anyone had told Ruth Watson about her relationship with George.

"You gonna be OK?"

"Will you stop asking me that?" Grace forced a smile to soften her comment.

Mary raised both hands in surrender. "Right. Just asking."

Grace supposed that George would be taking all his meals at home from now on. She was, therefore, surprised when he turned up at lunchtime with his wife.

There was no choice but for Grace to wait on them and suffer the inquisitive glances in their direction. Grace poured their coffee with a trembling hand. "Are you ready to order?"

"I think I'll have today's special," Ruth said with a smile. "Oh, I don't think we've met before." She offered her hand. "I'm Ruth Watson."

"This is Grace Irwin," George stammered. "She's helping Mary out for the summer."

Grace surmised, from the way he was acting, that he hadn't said anything to his wife about them.

"How nice. Are you here with your husband?" Ruth enquired.

"Er, no. I'm here by myself," Grace stuttered. She didn't want to have to deal with any more uncomfortable questions from Ruth, so she directed her next question to George. "Have you decided what you want yet?"

"I think I'll have the special as well," he said, toying with the silverware.

Grace hurried away to fill their order. She was frazzled throughout the rest of the lunch hour. She knew it was only a matter of time before Mrs. Watson heard the rumours about George and herself.

"How'd it go?" Mary asked after the lunch crowd dispersed.

"She seems nice," Grace said noncommittally.

"She is nice; so are you. You know it's only a matter of time before she finds out about you and George. What are you gonna do?"

"I don't know. I've never been in a situation like this before."

"It would be better if you were the one to tell her."

"I know that," Grace said gruffly. "And I will, when the time is right."

"I wouldn't wait too long if I were you."

Grace glared at her friend. "I know that too. Don't worry, I'll handle it when I'm ready."

"Sure kid," Mary said amidst the clatter of dishes.

"Did you hear the news?" The other waitress, Betty asked when she walked into the kitchen later that day to put the day's sales into the safe.

The two women paused in the middle of their respective chores.

"Ruth Watson was just telling me that Sarah Swift died of cancer last week."

"Are you sure?" Mary wanted to know.

"Of course I'm sure. Ruth was at the funeral and everything. You remember, they used to live around here?"

"I remember," said Mary.

"Hey, wait a minute. Didn't Sarah's family used to live in your cabin?" Betty turned to a red-faced Grace.

Grace coughed to clear her throat, before she could speak. "I believe so."

Mary could see that the direction of the conversation was upsetting Grace. "That's enough gossip for now," Mary told Betty. "If you're done for the day, you'd better get on home to your family."

"Sure thing," Betty said, oblivious to the undercurrents floating around. She gathered her things in preparation for home.

"How do you suppose Mr. Franco is taking this?" Grace asked when Betty left.

"It's hard to say. Sarah's been gone for a long time. But why do you care?" Mary asked bluntly. "You don't even like the man."

"I can't help but think about that little episode with him yesterday. I wonder if it might have something to do with Sarah's death," Grace said.

"I think you're letting your imagination get carried away with you," Mary pointed out.

Grace sighed. "You're probably right."

Mary hugged her friend. "I know I'm right."

On her way home that night, Grace couldn't help but notice that things seemed quiet at the Trading Post.

* * * * * *

When Grace got home, she took a glass of wine down to the river to help her relax. It had the desired effect of calming her frayed nerves. She closed her eyes and drifted with the sounds of the river.

The distant rumble of a motor boat interrupted her idyll, however. She sighed. She really wasn't in the mood for company. As the boat pulled up to the dock, Grace could see that Ruth Watson piloted the small craft. Her heart thumped loudly in her chest, and the color drained from her face. Would this horrible day ever end? She forced herself to greet the other woman.

"Is there somewhere we can talk?" Ruth asked stiffly. "I don't want to risk speculation should anyone happen to pass by."

"Of course," Grace responded with a quiver in her voice and lead Mrs. Watson to the cabin on shaky legs. Once inside, Grace turned to face Ruth and waited.

"I imagine you know why I'm here?"

"I have a pretty good idea."

"How you must have been secretly laughing at me, when we met at the diner."

"I can assure you, I was far from laughing," Grace said with as much dignity as she could muster.

Ruth crossed her arms across her ample bosom. "So, what do you have to say for yourself?"

"Only that our time together was completely innocent."

"That doesn't explain why you were seen having dinner with my husband. And if that wasn't' bad enough, you were in my home at the time."

"Perhaps you should talk to your husband about all this," Grace suggested.

"I can assure you, I already have."

"And what did he say?"

"That the two of you have been studying history together."

"Do you believe him?

"I don't know what to believe. I went away to spend time with our daughter, thinking I had nothing to worry about, and I come home to this," she said, palms up.

"Your husband loves you. He told me so himself."

Ruth's eyes flickered. "You talked about me?"

"Oh dear," Grace said. "I seem to have said the wrong thing. We only spoke in general terms about where you were, and that he missed you. Well, I asked that. He didn't volunteer the information," Grace back pedaled.

"I see. Perhaps you can explain why it was that you two were seen kissing after dark on your front porch?"

"Your husband was here one night," Grace explained, then quickly realized her blunder. "I mean he stopped by, but that was only to tell me about the Champlain diaries he'd acquired."

"That does sound like something George would do," she admitted. "But it doesn't explain the kiss."

"That's because there was no kiss."

Ruth stood silently waiting for an explanation.

"I think what someone saw was your husband comforting me." Grace said.

"Is that supposed to make me feel better?" Ruth asked through tight lips.

"Oh dear, I do seem to making a mess of this." Grace stared blankly at the floor. "I'm not accustomed to being in a situation like this. I'm feeling a bit dazed." She wrung her hands together. "The truth is, the night George came over, I wasn't here — at least not right away. I got lost in the woods, you see. By the time I got back, it was dark. When I saw your husband, I was so relied to see a friendly face, I started to cry and somehow ended up in his arms. Oh dear, that sounds bad doesn't it," she babbled. "I mean, I didn't mean to go to him, I just did." She shrugged. "I think he was just as surprised as I was by the turn of events. But there was no kiss," she affirmed. There was an awkward silence between the two women. When Ruth's arms began to relax at her side, Grace felt hopeful. "You do believe me, don't you?"

There was a long pause before the other woman responded. "It seems I have little choice. My husband told me the same story. Besides, I know my husband, and there's nothing more important to him than his research. He'd forget all about propriety when it comes to sharing historical information."

Grace took a deep breath and said with a quiver in her voice, "Mrs. Watson, let me just say that I recently lost my own husband in March. I have absolutely no interest in other men beyond friendship."

Ruth looked closely into Grace's eyes and made a decision. "It seems there's been a misunderstanding. I suppose it's my own fault for being away so long."

Grace sniffled and turned away to gather herself. "Thank you," she sighed.

"I'll leave you to yourself now. I hope you understand that I had to know the truth."

"Of course. I admire your resolve."

"Well, thank you for that," Ruth said and turned to leave.

It wasn't until Grace heard the door close behind Mrs. Watson that Grace crumbled onto the nearest chair.

* * * * * *

"Grace Irwin, is that you?" Mary hollered when Grace arrived at work the next day.

Grace had a terrible feeling of foreboding, when she entered the kitchen. "What's wrong?"

"Henry Franco's gone missing," Mary said without preface.

"What? Are you sure?" Grace asked.

"Well, no-one's seen hide nor hair of him since yesterday. He doesn't answer the door, and he hasn't opened up shop. He's always there. People are startin' to wonder."

Grace's eyes darted around the kitchen. "Do you suppose...?"

"What? That this has something to do with Sarah's death?"

Grace shrugged with eyes and hands raised.

"Good God a 'mighty! So you think he's gone daft?"

"You've known him longer than I have. Is it possible?"

"Damned if I know," Mary said. "It's not like I had much to do with him. For all I know, he could be on a trip," Mary speculated.

"Then why all the drama?" Grace said in a frustrated tone.

"It's just strange, that's all -- him taking off like that without anyone knowing where he is."

"But not unheard of?" Grace asked, hoping for some definitive answer.

"It's a puzzle that's for damn sure," Mary said.

"Well, I don't suppose we can do anything about it now," Grace said and resolved to focus on her work during the rest of her shift.

XXV

Grace carried the bouquet of flowers into the kitchen. She was worn out after a long day at the diner, worrying about what could have happened to Henry Franco. The flowers Mary had given her went a long way to improve her mood. She arranged the posy in an empty jam jar and carried it to her window-seat. That's when she caught a flicker of movement from the bedroom doorway. "Who's there?" she called out in a tremulous voice.

A bulky form stepped into the doorway.

"You!" She gasped and dropped the make-shift vase with a crash. "How did you get in here?"

Franco waved a key in her face, causing Grace to surmise that the lock hadn't been changed after the original owners sold the place.

Henry Franco didn't look his usual self. He hadn't shaved, his clothes looked like he'd slept in them, and what little hair he had stood on end in the parody of a mad man. But it was his eyes that frightened her the most. They had a wild faraway look in them — like he wasn't fully present. "Look, I know you don't like me Mr. Franco..."

"You used to call me Frankie." He slurred the words and stumbled toward Grace.

She stepped back. "What?"

"See this?" Franco held out his hand.

Grace was puzzled. "It's a rock."

"I kept it all this time."

"You did?"

"You gave it to me — said it reminded you of how strong I am. But I'm not strong, Sarah – not without you," he sputtered. "We had plans you and me. You ruined all that when you left. Why did you do it Sarah? Why did you leave me? I loved you."

Grace decided to play along until she could figure out what to do. "I er... had no choice."

"You said you'd marry me."

"My parents..." Grace prevaricated.

"Your parents said I weren't good enough for you coz I'm white." He pounded his chest. "Well, let me tell you something little girl," he growled from his greater height. "They were lucky I wanted to marry you."

Grace recoiled when she felt his spittle land on her face.

"Did they know you was carrying my baby?"

Grace gasped.

Franco stumbled backward and landed against a wall, where he braced himself. "You didn't tell them that did you? If they'd a known, they would a done different."

"I'm sorry," was all Grace could think to say.

"You kept my son from me." He swiped his arm over his eyes. "I seen him though, I did. In the school yard. Looks just like me, he does. What did you name him?" He turned to Grace.

Grace frantically searched her mind. "I called him er...John."

"John. That's a good name."

In an attempt to bring him back to the present with a more sane dialogue, Grace said, "You did all right though didn't you? You married and had other children."

"It weren't the same."

Grace had to keep him talking. "What about the girls?"

He took a menacing step toward her. "I wanted my son -- someone to carry on my name. Whose gonna look after the shop when I'm gone, huh? Them girls don't give a god damn about the shop."

Grace stepped back, but she wasn't fast enough.

Franco grabbed her by the arms and shook her until she became dazed. "You took my son," he cried.

"You're hurting me," Grace whimpered, but Franco couldn't hear her plea.

"I would a given you everything." He shoved Grace hard, and she lost her balance and landed across the room.

She scrambled into the corner. "Let me go."

"I can't."

Grace's spoke with a quiver in her voice. "If you hurt me, you'll only make things worse."

"Nothing could be worse than this," he groaned.

"I'll see you in jail if you so much as touch me again," Grace shrieked.

"Whatayamean? You'd never do such a thing."

"I'm not Sarah," Grace declared decisively.

Franco stumbled backwards shaking his head. "A 'course you are. This here's your house ain't it?"

"But I'm not Sarah. Sarah's gone."

"You're talking crazy." Franco spun clumsily.

"Don't you remember? Sarah died."

"Nooo!"

Grace watched in horror as Henry tripped over his feet, fell to his hands and knees, and started to cry. His whole body shook with his deep wracking sobs. His suffering pulled at her maternal instincts. She crawled closer, and reached out a tentative hand to him, then pulled back. She touched him. "I'm so..."

"Aaaaaagh!" Franco roared and swung his burly arm in a huge arch that sent Grace careening across the floor. She landed with a sickening thud against the wall. She rolled into a ball and waited for the next blow. But it didn't come. She lifted her head in time to see Henry Franco lurch for the door. She could hear his snuffles as he fumbled with the latch. When it finally gave, he disappeared into the night.

Grace scurried across the floor to shut and bolt the door behind the grief-stricken man. She leaned her weight against it, afraid he might change his mind and come back. Then she heard his motor boat on the river. She dared to peek out of the window, where she watched him ride away.

She had no idea where he had hidden his craft, or how he managed to maneuver it. She didn't care. He was gone.

Grace shuffled over to the broken glass and cut herself when she bent down to pick it up. "Ouch!" She brought the offending digit to her mouth, sank to the floor, and cried until she thought she was going to be sick.

With a hiccupping breath, Grace stumbled to the dresser drawer for a handkerchief. She shook out the neatly ironed square to dry her tears, when she caught her reflection in the mirror. Her eyes were red and swollen, and her face was blotchy. But that was the least of her worries. She sat on the bed and wondered what to do.

She was in no shape to venture out onto the river. Besides, she didn't want to risk running into Franco again tonight. She thought about going to Maggie's but didn't think she could manage it right now. And of course there was no phone to call for help. She'd just have to wait until morning to report the incident. But how did you deal with a man who was grieving? She had no idea. She decided to tackle what she could. She cleared away the broken glass and dumped it in the garbage. At least, in this, she had some control. With a shaky hand, she pulled out her journal, from its new hiding place in the dresser, and began to write.

Dear Charles: July 29, 1963

I don't know how I'm writing this after what's happened tonight. But I have to talk to someone. I can't sleep for fear of Franco coming back. I've never seen a man so out of his mind with grief. I thought maybe there was some aspect of good in him, until tonight. Now I'm not so sure. How dare he come into my home and frighten me like that? I've never done anything to him, unless you count the fact that I made friends with Mary and James. It's not my fault that the woman he loved left him for another man. He has no right.

What made me think I could live alone? It's obvious after tonight that it's not safe for a woman in a world of men. It's not fair. Why do men always think that just because they're bigger, stronger, and can yell louder, it gives them cause to do whatever they damn well please? Now the man has got me swearing. I hardly ever swear. Who does he think he is? Everyone loses a loved one at some time or other. You don't see them taking it out on someone else. Damn! Christ! Shit! I could scream, I'm so mad. I'd like nothing better than to go outside and let off some steam, but I don't trust him. He's out of his mind.

You want to know something crazy? I was starting to think I was doing all right on my own. Now I don't know what to do. Help me.

Grace.

Grace was emotionally and physically tired, yet she didn't think she could sleep. She wandered around the cabin to check that the windows were secure, and the door was still locked. As an extra measure of precaution, she stuck a kitchen chair under the door knob. She didn't know if it would work or not, but she'd seen it done in a movie to some effect. At least if someone tried to get in, the chair would tip over and alert her of impending danger. When she felt certain she'd done all she could, she went back to bed and tried to read.

But her mind kept going over the events of the evening causing knots in her stomach. Then the singing started. But it wasn't coming from the river this time. It was coming from inside her head. It was eerie and comforting at the same time. But more importantly, it lulled her to sleep.

XXVI

Grace's unread book fell to the floor. She placed it on the bedside table and went into the main part of the house to look around. It was hard to imagine that anything sinister had happened here the night before. However, she wasn't likely to forget the events that had left her feeling all jittery inside. She wandered around the room to check the windows and door. Satisfied that all was secure, she began her morning ablutions.

When she was done her morning coffee, she debated whether or not to venture outdoors. Maybe she should stay home and do some cleaning.

She scrubbed and polished and seethed. It made her angry to think that she'd let Henry Franco be the cause of her misery one more time. That he was out of his mind with grief was clear, but why did he have to take it out on her? She had come to the French River for some peace. She thought she had found it, but apparently she was mistaken. Maybe she should go back to Toronto, where she could feel safe again. She jumped when her ravings were interrupted by a knock at the door. But she quickly calmed herself, when she heard Maggie call out.

"What's going on here?" Maggie wanted to know when she saw the disarray.

"I'm cleaning."

"That much is obvious. What I want to know is why? Didn't you just give this place a good cleaning?"

"Well, I'm doing it again." Grace's lips trembled. She turned away so Maggie couldn't see her face.

"OK, what's going on?"

"Nothing," Grace stammered.

"I thought we already established that you're not a very good liar," Maggie pointed out. "So, why don't you just get it over with, and tell me what the hell's happened since the last time I saw you."

Grace stared past Maggie. "I was thinking it might be time for me to go back home, that's all."

"I thought you had the place until the end of the summer."

"I changed my mind."

"What? I don't understand. Did you have a falling out with Mary?"

"No, it's just time for me to go. I've told you before, I don't belong here."

"You can pull that nonsense on someone else," Maggie said and grabbed Grace by the arms.

"Oh, you're hurting me." Grace rubbed her sore arms.

"I didn't grab you that hard," Maggie said. "Something has clearly upset you. I'm not leaving until you tell me why you're acting so strange. Why are you talking about leaving?"

Grace's lips began to quiver, and her eyes watered. She looked up at her friend. It was her undoing. She dropped her head into her hands and released all the tension she'd been feeling since Franco's unwelcome visit the night before.

"There, there." Maggie held her friend and offered words of comfort. "Let it all out. It will make you feel better. Then you can tell me what's going on. Can you do that?"

Grace sniffled and nodded. She felt so safe in this woman's arms. Why couldn't she be more like Maggie who was strong and capable enough to take care of her own problems without bothering someone else?

"Let's go sit on the couch, so we'll be more comfortable. Now tell me what's got you so upset?" Maggie said when Grace's sobs subsided to mere hiccups.

Grace told Maggie about Franco's unwelcome visit, how he had mistaken her for Sarah, and how he started ranting about his feelings. "Did you know Sarah was pregnant with his child?"

"Oh Lord."

Fresh tears appeared in Grace's eyes. "Then he hurt me."

"He didn't...?"

Grace shook her head. "No, not that. But he was so out of his mind with grief that he grabbed me by the arms and shook me so hard I fell."

"So that's why you cried out when I grabbed you," Maggie said absentmindedly.

"He kept calling me Sarah," Grace said.

"Oh dear. I had no idea he would take her death so hard. I was sure he'd be over Sarah by now. It all happened so long ago."

"Maybe that's why he's made my life so difficult since I got here. Somehow, my being here has stirred up all that old hurt."

Maggie glanced around the room. "Do you mean to say that because you're living in Sarah's house he's transferred all his pent up feelings for her onto you?"

"It's a thought," Grace shrugged. "It might also explain why he objected to my friendship with Mary."

Maggie frowned. "I don't follow."

"Well, last night he told me Sarah's family didn't think he was good enough for her, because he's white. Yet, here I stand — a white woman who's friends with a Native woman."

"Oh, now I see what you're getting at," Maggie said. "You've been able to accomplish what he couldn't."

"Exactly."

Maggie slid back on the couch to consider the notion. "I never imagined that Henry was so tortured."

"Grief can do strange things to people."

"That it does, but still. He went too far. You have to tell the police."

"Tell them what?"

"That this man attacked you." Maggie stated the obvious.

"And what of his motivation? The man was grieving. Does he deserve to be punished for that?"

"That's not for you to decide. His actions, whatever his motivation, have hurt you."

"He was grieving," Grace said quietly. "I did a few stupid things myself when Charles died."

"So you plan on letting him force you out of this new life you've built for yourself?"

"I've made such a mess things anyway. I'll probably be better off in Toronto," she shrugged.

"What the hell are you talking about?"

"Since I arrived, I've not only managed to stir up things for Mr. Franco, I've been branded a hussy by the locals, and accused of dealing in spirits. I'm not exactly off to a rousing start in my new life. I keep telling you, I don't belong here."

"Did you really think it was going to be easy?" Maggie rebuked.

"I think it's time for me to leave."

Exasperated now, Maggie said, "Well, I don't know what else to say. You clearly seem determined to punish yourself for someone else's actions. If you're firmly resolved about leaving, I guess I can't stop you."

"Exactly."

"Are you at least going to say goodbye to Mary and the boys before you go?"

"Of course I will," Grace said with a sinking feeling.

"Will you be back?"

"I don't know." The tears started to well up again.

"Well, hells bells. I don't know what to make of all of this," Maggie said, shaking her head.

"I've decided to return home early that's all."

"I think you're making a big mistake, you know."

"I appreciate your concern, but it's my mistake to make," Grace said.

"So I guess this is likely goodbye," Maggie said sadly. She gave Grace a fierce hug. "Promise me one thing. Promise me you'll think about going to the police."

"I have a feeling I won't hear the end of it, unless I agree." Grace gave in with a sigh.

"Well good. I guess that will have to be enough."

"I don't know if I can say goodbye to Mary personally. If I wrote her a letter, would you give it to her?"

"This is going to break her heart. The least you could do is say goodbye in person."

"Will you do it?" Grace pleaded.

"I don't think I will," Maggie replied, stubbornly. "I may have agreed to adhere to your wishes about leaving, but I'll be damned if I'll make it easy for you. Tell her yourself." She spun on her heel and shot out the door.

With a heavy heart, Grace started to pack. There were still a few items that would have to wait until morning, but that wouldn't take long.

She didn't sleep well that night. Every sound startled her. But it was more than that. Was Maggie right? Was she giving up too soon? There was a big part of her that wanted to stay, but she was afraid she'd already failed to make a life for herself without Charles, afraid of facing Mr. Franco again, and afraid of going to the police. Surely it was better to go back to the world she knew in Toronto. At least she'd feel safe there. She'd had too many sleepless nights since she'd arrived. It would be good to sleep without worry or fear. She wondered about how she was going to say goodbye to Mary.

XXVII

Some unknown impulse brought Grace fully awake during the early morning hours. She climbed out of bed and moved quietly around her rooms, fearful that Mr. Franco might be lurking about. Finding nothing that could account for her disquiet, she wandered over to the picture window and saw a ghostly mist hanging over the river.

Inexplicably drawn to the mystical sight, she grabbed the quilt from the back of the couch and wrapped it around her shoulders. The haze parted around her feet, as she slipped down to the river bank.

An incandescent light emanated from the rolling mist. But rather than feeling afraid, she felt comforted by the sight. She knew she would miss this place with a certainty she couldn't explain. Despite what happened with Mr. Franco, being here had changed her. While she was still afraid that staying would only cause more trouble, there was a part of her that was ashamed and angry with herself for running away. But what else could she do? She'd made trouble for George, and although that little incident seemed to be cleared up, her reputation was tainted. Then there was the issue of Henry Franco. Her presence caused old hurts to surface, and they were directed at her. She didn't think she could face another altercation with that man.

Then she heard the familiar melody that had come to mean so much to her. It floated across the mist, to where she stood beside the river bank. She heard the gentle splash of paddles sliding into the water, before an apparition appeared out of the haze. She held her breath, as a creamy opalescent bow of an enormous birch-bark canoe cut through the mist and floated toward her in slow motion. Her heartbeat thudded in her chest, and her body became heated in the chill morning air. She couldn't move. The vision became larger with every swish of its brightly painted paddles, as they dipped into the shadowy depths of the French River.

Her brain tried to make sense of the fact that the craft was filled with hardy French-Canadian voyageurs. Some had bright sashes around their waist, but they all wore rough homespun clothes of various colors. Their head-gear consisted of a toque, beaver hat, or a bandana tied around the head to keep unruly hair off sun-roughened faces.

She took in every detail as it got closer and closer. Just when she thought it was going to ram right into the dock, it swung away at the very last minute giving her a full view of the immense craft. It must have been at least thirty feet in length and five or six feet at its deepest point in the center. Its curved shape was higher in the front and back and concave in the center. The sides were stained a burnt umber and seemed to be divided into panels from the bow to stern. She recognized it as a Canot de Maitre' by the number of men and large cargo it carried.

As it drifted back into the mist, she became aware of a man standing in the stern waving goodbye. "Charles!" She reached out to him, but he faded into the mist along with the canoe.

She sat down and tried to calm her beating heart. She wiped her hands on the quilt and attempted to make sense out of the vision. She didn't move again until the sun appeared on the horizon and melted the mist away. Birds celebrated a new day, and now she could too. She knew what she had to do. She went back into the cabin to unpack.

Study Questions

How did the relationships between: 1) Grace and Mary and 2) Grace and Maggie, help to change Grace? Have you ever had such a friendship with another person?

What is the significance of the river in *River of the Stick Wavers*?

Do you think that Henry Franco was justified in is feelings toward Grace? Why or why not?

The mythical singing that Grace heard is integral to the story. What do you think is the significance of the singing?

How did the history of the voyageurs help Grace to change?

Did you think, or hope, that there was an intimate connection between Grace and George? Would it have added anything to the story? Why?

Grace felt a strong connection with her landscape. Do you think it's possible for a person to have this kind of connection? Why?

James seemed very comfortable in his own skin. He had no illusions about his place in the world. Why do you think this is? What would it take for you to feel content with who you are and your place in the world?

The female characters in this story are all strong women (whether they realize it or not). Based on your own experience, how would you define what constitutes a strong woman?

Did you find the end of this story satisfying? Why or why not?

Did you understand why Grace decided to stay at the French River?

This book talks about the many ways people deal with death. If you feel comfortable, talk about the different ways people have dealt with death and grief in your own life.

Printed in Canada